Redemption

Fallen Angel Series Book 2

Renee Pace

DEDICATION

There are so many angels walking among us who slay their own demons, defend people without a second thought while keeping the faith of kindness. This book is for you.

CHAPTER ONE

S hea clutched the blanket tight to her shivering frame, praying for solitude or a way to end the ache etched deep within her. She stood as straight as she could, hidden behind the long red curtain concealing her bedroom window. In the dark of her room and with only the sliver of a moon shining through the cloud-covered Boston harbor, she was awash in gray shadows. The angle of her stance allowed her to easily observe the night's scenery. And night, not day, had lately become her favorite time. A month ago, not the case. Sun streaming from the Heavens used to make her smile. Now it beckoned tears.

As usual she found solace nestled in the shadows of her room. She had no reason to be cold. Her bedroom heat had been cranked up earlier and a roaring fire toasted the room, yet not enough warmth penetrated her body these days. Well, that wasn't entirely true. Heat soaked through her cells when she least wanted or desired it, alarming her. Her gaze once again turned to the mirror by her dresser.

As always, her new look shocked her. Her blonde hair, now as black as demon wings, mocked her. Shea hated her hair.

When she first woke, two weeks ago, and discovered her change, she'd mustered her courage and hacked off her long strands. It hadn't mattered. She was cursed. Her hair had grown back overnight, long thick and eerily black—a stamp to all her Cherub sisters of what had befallen her. A white streak of hair ran in the middle of her hairline. Her sisters had not said a word to her of it. To speak of her ill; her falling into disrepute was not their way.

Willing a calm, she never felt these days, Shea tried once again to reach out to her twin. As usual the voice which had been her constant companion was now empty. Tears ran unchecked down her cheeks and the willpower to wipe them away seemed useless. The heat of arms Shea didn't want to welcome, didn't want to acknowledge, slid around her with ease. Deliberately, she fought not to move, even while she yearned to lean a fraction back into his heated embrace. To do so would acknowledge his power. Shea could not acquiesce to his hold on her.

He didn't speak, or demand answers. Nor did he ask questions; telling in itself. He knew what her heart and soul ached for. He knew she was now lost to the world she had been born into and nothing could change her path. And all because of him. It was always good for Shea to ground her thoughts with his wants, his demands and the curse of the consequences which had befallen her.

"I will make this right," he said.

His hot breath on the back of her neck, even though her long thick hair covered her flesh, sent a cascade of goosebumps over her flesh. Shea told herself it wasn't desire, and even that self-inflicted lie left a sour taste in her mouth.

His arms pulled her tighter to his muscled frame. But Shea knew if she turned around he would be invisible. He liked to camouflage the night with his body. Deep down he didn't want her to see him in his true form—demon. She'd cursed him enough the first few nights he thought to offer comfort. Shea wondered if her words wounded him. Heavenly doubtful. He's a demon. He used me to get what he wanted. He took from me my power and now because of him, I no longer hear my sister.

There was a niggling thought that she had known the consequences of her actions, but the power for answers overrode common sense.

For a moment Shea thought of the irony of her life. She truly had become a fallen angel and now thanks to Lucifer's son, was even more cursed. Who would have thought it possible? Certainly not Shea when she'd willingly taken up arms in Isabella's fight for Cherub independence. Of course, Shea's motives were much more selfishly driven. She had thought independence would enable her to free her twin. But alas, it had proven to be a foolish desire. The only thing she'd done was to cause more strife to her beloved sister. A sister who not once had Shea had the privilege of seeing or had even dared to acknowledge. From their first heavenly breaths, they had shared a special bond. They were telepathically linked. But the one soul for one person rule of the Heavens, citied angel twins didn't exist. Or so she'd been told since the beginning of her Cherub teachings. Lies. All of it. Even at a young age, Shea had known it best to keep her secret sealed.

"Trust me. I will make this right for you and her."

The confidence of his words should have been a warning to Shea but that lonely feeling she'd been trying to hide from her fellow sisters was too much for her to bear. She had never been strong like Isabella or Meredith. She never had reason before.

Shea turned, his arms sliding slightly away, allowing her to melt more into his embrace; conceding to her hidden desire. "I want you to let me go."

"Never."

It was the same argument they played with each other nightly. He, her invisible demon who only dared to darken her room when the night's shadows allowed him privacy, and she, the cursed fallen angel who felt more useless by the blessed prayer bells.

His lips when they found her mouth were soft and questing. Shea did not bend. She kept her distance. She didn't deserve to feel when the anxiety of what she had lost, of what she feared, darkened her mind more and more. What if her sister had died? What if his taking her power had doomed her sister more?

Shea subtly moved. He finally released his hold on her to allow her to take one step away. She knew he looked at her but the same could not be said of her.

"Show yourself."

He laughed, the sound dark, rich and lush. She liked it but bit her tongue before speaking such.

"Why? So, you can curse my demon form again?"

Shea found herself smiling. Her words held power over him. She tucked the information deep inside. "I will hold my tongue. I have need to speak to you face to face."

The words were no sooner said than his solid form materialized an inch from her. Shea couldn't help herself. As always his beauty took her breath away. Sinfully ironic. His eyes, the color of dark melted chocolate, were direct and assessing. He took a step back, allowing her to inspect him further should she wish to do so. Shea did. That too she couldn't help. He wore dark jeans, a black shirt and a black leather jacket. His wavy charcoal-colored hair teased the tips of his ears and was slightly longer than she recalled.

"Do I meet with your approval?" he asked, mockingly but Shea caught the hint of vulnerability.

"I am sorry I called you names."

"No, you are not. Do not lie to me Shea, for I will taste your lies. There are no secrets between us."

My whole existence has been a secret. Stilling her thoughts, Shea gulped. "Will you help me?"

He lowered himself to his knees, the sight beguiling her senses. She wanted to tell him to get up off the hard, wooden floor of her room but knew he wouldn't.

"You are my b'iã. My chosen one. I will do all within my power to make you happy."

The words she knew he'd say. The words she'd hoped and didn't dare pray for because what she was about to ask, she could bequeath no other.

Dropping to her knees so for once they were both keenly aware of how well they matched each other, Shea spoke what needed to be said. "Save her."

She didn't need to voice the rest. As always he knew. He bowed his head slightly. "For you anything. Thy will be done. I will return with the want of your heart but I demand something in exchange for this burden you have asked of me."

By the holy scribes, I did not anticipate this. Feeling as if her throat was parched, Shea found her courage. "Haven't you taken from me enough?"

For a moment a look of anguish and regret flitted across his too-handsome proud looking features. His eyes bespoke power and her destiny, and Shea wished for a second she had not bothered him with the desire of her heart.

"We are not having that discussion again, for you and I will always disagree on the motivation. You are asking me to risk life and limb, to venture to your Heavens, when you know I am demon. If they find me, I will be killed. What I demand is simple. You."

Shea did gasp this time. He couldn't possibly mean what I think he does. Biting her lip, she tasted the coppery scent of blood, liking it a little too much. "I need clarification for what you are asking of me."

His right eyebrow rose slightly, almost like he approved of her testing the terms of their agreement.

"Do you? You know perfectly well what I am asking. I want a night with you. To be even more specific. A night in your bed with you. Is that too much to ask of my b'iã?"

Shea fought not to cringe. She hated that word. Hated how much power was behind such a simple three-letter word. She was his b'iã and as much as she fought against it and would continue to fight against the bonds weaving them together, she knew in her heart she'd cave to his demands. She'd do anything for her sister.

"Fine. Bring my sister to me and your demand will be met."

He chuckled again. "We are not so dissimilar, Shea. I will do as you have asked. In my absence think fondly of me."

Shea couldn't help herself. She snorted on her laugh. "Think fondly of you..."

It was on the tip of her tongue to say the word 'demon' and like he knew it, and he probably did, he simply smiled at her. By the blessed path of light, no demon should look that good smiling. Shea wisely kept her thoughts to herself.

Being born into the Heavens, the meaning of sacrifice was an integral part of life's purpose. All Cherubs were taught from the moment they walked that will and sacrifice were part and parcel of the Almighty's paths. After all, a Cherub's whole existence was one of sacrificing for another. The Mistress chose the Seraphim to be their mates and love had nothing to do with the Oracle's terms binding them for eternity. While Shea didn't have a Seraphim warrior to cater to, it appeared by the blessing of the Mistress that she did have a demon. If her demon would do what she knew no Seraphim would dare, then so be it.

She'd sacrifice anything and everything for her sister. Sacrifices were nothing new for Shea. Her whole life she'd learned to do without to help in some small way for her sister and if she had to bleed or give into the demon's demands she'd willingly do so. After all, her life mattered naught anymore.

CHAPTER TWO

A sh knew she'd ask. Still, he had wanted her to beg and plead her case. What he hadn't anticipated were tears, or how those damn silent tears of hers would rip out his demon-crusted heart. She'd changed him. He wondered if she knew the power she now wielded over him like a sword created from the Archangel Gabriel himself. Ash prayed she remained ignorant of her hold. He laughed inwardly at his own thoughts.

Prayers were for the weak and wouldn't bring him victory. It was not like the Mistress wanted anything to do with him, but it appeared as if their paths were becoming more intertwined. He hated her for that and for many other reasons. Reasons he suspected but didn't want to know. The Mistress had come to him in haunting dreams, detailing a life in the Heavens that had left him with longing for something he couldn't have. What had Ash done? He'd lived her torment daily, and ignored her pleas. After all, she'd ignored him for years. Bound to his father's realm, he knew he hadn't the power to break free from Lucifer's hold so Ash had plotted and waited. Patience; a learned habit. He might have loathed it, especially when his father felt he needed another lesson in discipline to understand his role in the world. Ash had never once spoken his desire for more than a demon's life and that alone saved him from Lucifer's endless desire to reclaim the Heavens.

He waited until almost dawn before daring to leave the brownstone. Ash had been using up a lot of his power by taking over the human the Cherubs called Gareth, but he did what had to be done. Isabella and Nathanael would not take kindly to letting a demon enter their sanctuary, but Ash couldn't go without seeing Shea. Their bond had settled deep within him and not for the first time Ash wondered if he had a soul. At night he put Gareth's human form to sleep and willed his demon essence to Shea's room. She knew he was there. She might not always acknowledge him but when his shadow-filled arms held her, she didn't fight. Ash liked to think it a good sign. Tonight, he'd gained her trust. He'd do the one impossible task she asked of him and in all likelihood die. Somehow, the taste of death no longer mattered.

However, Ash was not a fool. He hadn't survived the years in Hell with his father for nothing. Knowledge in this case would be helpful. The only person who could help him was the Mistress, who he hated on equal footing with his father.

Using the dark clouds as cover, Ash rounded the corner of the recreational center, catching dark shadows in the corner of the alley. He waited and smiled. Two teens were going at it like Hell-bats, too intent on their own pleasure. He could easily flick a light on to scare them but he needed quiet. He strolled farther down the deserted street, the stench of brine and oil permeating the air the closer he got to Boston's harbor. Slipping into a deserted warehouse, one of many dotting the landscape, which had been thriving at one time as an industrial hub, he focused his thoughts.

After ten minutes with a no-show and realizing the call of dawn would herald more people and weaken him further, Ash tisked. The Mistress damn well knew he was calling her but she liked to make him and all those she served wait. Well, he didn't have time for her games. Ash did what had to be done.

Using gloves, he held the small holy dagger he'd sequestered, okay stolen, from Isabella's room and winced in pain as he forcibly used the tip to make the sign of the crucifix over his heart. Often, Ash thought it ironic that humans viewed the cross as a religious symbol when in truth it was completely symbolic with his father's realm.

With blood now freely dripping down his chest he stated his demands. "Show thyself Mistress. I don't have all day for this." Speaking Scripture never sat well with him but the power of the words, along with his blood-sacrifice, would be answered.

"Thy reverence has always pleased me," said the Mistress.

Her voice came from his back. Shivers knifed through his skin. Ash, like any good warrior, never liked to give his opponent his back. To turn, though, would acknowledge how he felt, so Ash forced himself not to flinch even as she moved closer. The rustle of her heavy robes sliding along the dirt-crusted cement floor of the warehouse reminded him of the scurry of rats, a sound he'd come to detest since spending five years in his own hole as punishment for daring to openly question his father.

"I need information," stated Ash.

"Information is not for the faint of heart. And the path thee have set upon does not demand I answer to thy quest."

This time Ash turned to face her. As always she was covered head to toe, literally in her black robes. Not a speck of flesh showed. Even the thick mesh covering over her face carefully obscured what one would seek—her eyes. "I am the only one you have to help you negotiate with my father."

"Do not think thyself indispensable."

Okay, Ash tried a different tactic. She, as ever, was difficult to deal with. "I seek to find someone, an angel who in the heavenly realm does not exist."

The only show he'd caught her attention was the slight cocking to one side of her head. So slight, Ash might have mistaken it but he'd venture not. She wondered too what he sought, even while thinking she knew everything that went on in the Heavens. Ash was not about to play her game.

Staring at her, he notched up his chin. "Don't play coy with me. You are omniscient and know all in the Heavens. The one I seek is Shea's twin."

"There are no angel twins. An angel can only have one soul."

Ash took a step forward. "Tell that lie to yourself enough times Mistress and you might believe it, but the truth is bitter and foul tasting and you know it. Twins have been born in your Heaven before as history has stated and clearly recorded."

"Your father was an abomination."

"No. When he was birthed he was innocent to the evil ways but only with the discovery of what you are once again trying to say does not exist, did he turn." And who wouldn't? Ash had grown up with stories about his father's discovery, of how they'd kept his twin brother chained for a millennium. How Lucifer had been the one to finally save him only to watch as his twin took the angel's dagger to kill himself. Suicide. It had been the first weakening of the heavenly walls of purity and Lucifer had snapped and turned. Still to this day, Ash felt as if his father held himself responsible.

"Demon, you are not listening. The Heavens do not allow a twin to live. The first to take the heavenly breath lives, the other dies. It is now a heavenly blood-ordained law."

Nice law in that Heaven of yours. Wisely, Ash kept his mouth shut, trying to absorb what she was truly telling him. For in his heart, he knew Shea's twin was alive. Obviously though the Mistress did not. However, one could never tell with her. She played games much like his father and he was not about to be her pawn, or scapegoat.

"What if you are wrong? What if one lives? Where would she be?"

The Mistress stepped back and went still and silent. It was an eerie move Ash would have liked to master.

"I hear the truth behind what you believe but I see no twin in the Heavens."

"Again, where could one hide an angel?"

"In The Precipice. The space beneath the heavenly realm where there is no power, but a vast emptiness of nothing. It would not make sense to keep one such as you have stated. To what purpose?"

The Mistress wasn't voicing anything he hadn't thought. What would be the purpose of keeping Shea's sister alive? None that he could think of.

"Shea firmly believes in this truth?"

A question. The Mistress was asking him a question? That was not the norm of things. "She speaks the truth."

"Then I must attend her."

Oh shit. He didn't want that. "Leave her alone. I take care of her now as is my right. You made sure of that."

She nodded. "I did what you asked. The course thee had set forth meant freedom from your father's realm. Is that not what you fought for?"

Of course, he wanted that. Did he though expect to be bound to a Cherub? Did he think for one demon second he'd care for her feelings more than his quest? Hell no. She had known what would happen. Ash wanted to hate her for the scope of her omission. "Shea is mine to comfort and I will keep my promise to her. This has been a waste of time."

"Time, demon is never wasted. You have learned where Shea's twin might be held and I have learned a most important discovery."

"And that would be?"

"My secret, not yours." She vanished with those ominous telling words. Ash knew though what she meant. She had thought to know all in the Heavens but it appeared someone had sneaked something by her. Shea's twin. But why?

Ash needed to know more. The Precipice. The only place to learn more information about the nothing place was back with the Cherubs. He'd assume Gareth's form and use Meredith to get more intel. Then he'd mass an army and get what Shea sought. Anything to keep those damn tears of hers from falling.

CHAPTER THREE

D awn crested through Meredith's open window. She loved the filtering sunlight tenderly streaming through her bow window. This was her moment of peace. In another half hour, Izzy, her best friend and fellow warrior would probably barge in and demand for her to arrange another weapons training session with the six earth-born angels. Meredith fought to keep her peaceful feeling. The thought of dealing with the earth-born angels made Meredith long to pull up her blankets and hide from the day. Would this be an indulgence in sloth? If so, she'd take the penance if it kept her free from dealing with them. They were so unangelic, Meredith found herself questioning the Almighty's wisdom for their existence. A blasphemous thought but still she couldn't suppress it.

The smell of pancakes hit her and she moaned. While her task might be dealing with the earth-bound angels, each of her fellow Cherubs had their own assigned duties in this realm. And every day as she tasted another one of

Nayla's concoctions, she thanked her heavenly bells she'd joined them in their exile. If she had to suffer in exile at least her stomach didn't have to.

"It's hopeless," declared Izzy, marching into Meredith's room, as usual without knocking. Meredith resisted rolling her eyes. She had always hated that human emphasis from the teens who frequented the recreational center. Now, however, Meredith understood why they did it.

Meredith walked into her bathroom and let Izzy have her morning rant. Lucky for her the sound of Izzy's irate voice got slightly muffled with the wooden door acting as a sound barrier. But it wouldn't be for long. Knowing she had to face her friend eventually, she quickly washed her face and braided her long hair to keep it out of the way.

Meredith opened the door and moved to her dresser.

"Meredith they are totally useless."

"I am sure you are exaggerating," said Meredith, pulling out her new attire. Black sweatpants and a t-shirt. Comfort clothing for the hand-to-hand combat she would soon be participating in.

Izzy flopped down on Meredith's unmade bed. "No, I'm not. What was I thinking? We can't train them. They don't have a clue what they will be facing. None of them have ever seen a demon and when I start to talk about them, they all but roll their eyes at me, like I'm the one lying. And seriously, there are only six of them. Six against a demon army." Izzy placed her head in her hands in frustration.

"These six will train more. We will have to make do with what we have."

Izzy's blue eyes turned on her sharply. "What we need is a demon."

"Now, Izzy that's impossible." But Meredith knew that falsehood and feared her friend was about to resort to drastic measures to get her point across. "Have you talked to Mike? He can help. Let him help. You are taking too much on and I'm sure Nathanael..."

"Oh, don't talk to me of him. I don't want to see him. You wouldn't believe what he asked of me."

Meredith knew exactly what Nathanael asked of Izzy and she liked his idea. Izzy, however, did not. "He is offering hope. You pointed out we need more warriors and we need help training them. What is the harm in what he is offering?"

Izzy practically flew off the bed. "Harm. Have you lost all your senses? More Seraphim? You would want to deal with more of his kind?"

Meredith laughed as she pulled her long nightgown over her head and began dressing for the day. Modesty, while highly valued as Cherubs was something she was becoming less inclined to deal with. "His kind, are our kind. Why do you feel the need to separate them? We are one. We are all angels."

"Are we? Sorry, I don't feel that way."

Meredith fought not to show any emotion. She too echoed Izzy's thoughts but didn't dare let on. What the Mistress asked of them seemed an impossible task. Maybe it was why she asked it of them—the forsaken ones. Dressed, Meredith sat down on her bed and urged Izzy to sit beside her.

"Maybe you are right. Let's work with what we have. Let Mike help. He should be the one dealing with them. I heard he's secured a separate training space for us."

Izzy notched up her chin and smiled. "By the blessed path, that would make me so happy. I'm sick and tired of trying to show these earth-born angels how to move like warriors in our common room. We truly do need a space where we can move and wield our weapons without fear of hurting each other. Still though, I think showing them a demon would do them a world of good."

"You may be correct, but let's ease into this slowly with them. I, for one, am discovering the longer I'm around them the more I like them. Even that girl, Willow, who has pierced her body in more areas than I thought possible."

Both of them laughed. The sound, carefree reminded Meredith how remiss she'd been lately. Izzy was their natural leader, the Cherub who had originally led them in arms to rebel for more than a Cherub existence. The sacrifices she'd taken on for them all could not be overlooked. Meredith was her support beam, her founding candle, the light of which helped to guide Izzy.

"Take a day off, Izzy. I will deal with Mike and the earth-born angels today."

"And what would you have me do?"

Meredith got up from her bed. "Well, I'm sure Nathanael can help you spend your time wisely."

A blush stole over her friend's face. "I really don't think I should see him today."

"Don't tell me you two are fighting again."

"No, it's not that. I mean, yes we're arguing about his offer to secure a way for his brethren to help but it's much more complicated than that."

At the door, Meredith waited for Izzy to continue and when it became clear she wasn't going to, Meredith sighed. "Izzy, you are his b'iã. Don't fight it."

"He agreed to the terms."

"Yes, but I do believe you are torturing both of yourselves unnecessarily. You have the Mistress' blessing."

"But I don't want it. I don't want to feel like he's with me because of this pre-ordained stuff we're tied to."

"Come on. After all you've been through you know what Nathanael feels for you is much more. Torment yourself all you want but he is Seraphim and your mate and sooner rather than later he might press his point."

A smile quirked briefly on Izzy's lips, before she sailed out of Meredith's room. In the hallway she looked at Meredith. "Maybe you are correct. I will do as you have advised. Today will be a day off from them. Thank you, Meredith."

Meredith nodded, feeling almost like that was too easy. About an hour later, after having eaten her fill of delicious pancakes, she understood why.

The group of six earth-born angels had taken over Mike's recreational center and he looked like he wanted to kill all of them. Music blared from someone's iPod with a disturbing erratic beat.

"It's the Sex Pistols," said Cole.

Meredith refrained from asking what or who that was. She didn't need to know, but as usual Cole liked to educate her.

"It's a band. They were popular about a decade ago. You've never heard of them, have you?"

"No. They are not something I would seek to listen to. And I think Mike would like for you to turn it down."

"Actually, he told me to turn it up. Said he had to curse loudly for a good two minutes and didn't want to be overheard." Cole laughed.

Meredith thought she'd made two people, who obviously were so opposed to laughing, chuckle in one morning. Again, Meredith found herself observing Cole. He like the other earth-born Sere who had offered to help fight the demons, felt at ease with weapons. She watched Cole turn down the iPod. He, like Devon, had hair that reached his shoulders. Where Devon had the traditional dark Sere hair, Cole's hair was almost the exact shade of Meredith's hair—wheat blonde and wavy. Unlike real angels though Cole's eyes were Earth-bound, the color of murky pond water, varying in shades from green to gray, depending on his moods. His arms were etched in Scripture speak and she read the text. "For thy love of the Almighty I pledge my heart, soul and body." She wondered if he knew the rest of the holy Scripture, for she most certainly did. "My will is not my own, my destiny is tied to all and I am bound for eternity as a mere slave to the Almighty's design. Blood willingly do I pledge."

It was the full Seraphim brethren code and the entire script had been etched on the back by the one who had dared to train Meredith and Izzy in the Heavens. The one Seraphim who, while begging them to not take up arms, had shown them with gruff commands how to do so properly. Meredith shook her head. She didn't want to think about him. He, like all Seraphim, was no more for her.

When questioned, Cole and Devon had said their comfort-zone was with the morning stars, and swords had come about by necessity. She had tried to find out why only they had come forward to help, when others from the Seraphim House wanted nothing to do with weapons, but like typical Sere they'd ignored her questions. Their tactic, diversion. They had set about to question her about her decade-long exile from the Heavens. Meredith had let them think she didn't know they hadn't answered, trying to not offend them, but she wondered why they were so secretive and not liked by their own brethren. Often Meredith thought it perplexing they didn't ask more about heavenly life. She wondered if they knew how much Earth and Heaven were dissimilar.

"This had best be the last day they use my place," said Mike, as he moved up beside her. Meredith looked at him. He had dark circles under his eyes and looked like he hadn't slept in two weeks. Probably a truth. Since the Mistress had declared that Izzy and Nathanael needed to recruit the earth-born angels Meredith suspected no one had slept. The task set upon them felt momentous.

"I take it your friend has allowed us to use his gym."

Mike winked at her. "Only after lots of negotiations."

Meredith found herself smiling for real. Mike, besides being Izzy's and all of their saviors, had over the years become a confidant of sorts. Now that he knew the truth of their existence, Meredith felt even more at ease around the six-foot four guy, who was built like a tank but had a heart as pure as heavenly wine.

"And what did you use for your leverage?" asked Meredith, accepting the coffee Mike was starting to pour for her from the bar. The recreational center was Mike's gift to the teens in need of a safe hang-out place in this part of Boston. Most nights of the week, Mike arranged entertainment, like their group known as the Minstrel

Singers who regularly performed on Friday and Saturday nights. If it wasn't them it would be open mike, comedy or talent night. Mike felt strongly teens needed a place to chill and his bouncers enforced the strict no drugs or alcohol rule inside the club but what happened outside, belonged to the dark of the night to claim.

Mike chuckled. "Beautiful young women who wanted to learn how to defend themselves. What guy could resist that?"

"What age is this friend of yours?"

Well, he's a few years younger than me."

"Exactly how many, Mike?"

Mike looked down at the floor. "Christ," said Mike, blushing. He did that regularly when he cursed. It always made him look younger. "He's nineteen. Inherited his brother's gym after he got killed in a freak accident."

"I feel your pain, Mike. Thank you from my heart for making this possible. But, this friend of yours might be alarmed when we start using swords and morning stars."

"Actually, he promised he'd stay away while we train. If I didn't do this, Meredith, your common room and my recreational center would be torn to bits. We need a good space to train. Nathanael looked it over and he agrees with the place."

Meredith nodded. Her eyes turned to the door when Gareth walked in. Today, he chose to ignore her. She felt hurt by his actions but refrained from pestering him. His need of her had diminished easily over the last few weeks but often it felt to Meredith something was lost in Gareth.

"Just ignore him. Lately he's been acting like a bear."

"I am sure he is concerned with the training schedule," said Meredith, taking a sip of the coffee Mike had brewed for her. His kindness touched her. He seemed to easily recall all of their favorite foods and drinks and this morning the three heaping teaspoons of sugar in her bitter coffee tasted sinfully delicious.

"Yeah, guess that's it. So, I gather that you're here to fill in for Izzy this morning."

"Most certainly. She needs a day of rest."

"Couldn't agree with you more. But I highly doubt she will rest. She and Nathanael were plotting something yesterday...something that sounded a lot like Nathanael asking for help from his brethren. Just what I freakin' need around here—more angels."

Meredith finished her drink and gave him a wry smile. "I believe that sentiment would be shared by Izzy. She is trying her best to thwart Nathanael's plans."

"Well, as much as I dislike more angels, Nathanael does have a point. This group needs a lot of work. And six against an army of demons is a suicide mission."

"I agree." Meredith watched as Gareth moved two chairs out of the way. The floor mats were already in place and she'd wasted enough time talking. Taking a last sip of the brew, Meredith moved into the middle of the room, nodded at Gareth, who still barely acknowledged her, and positioned the six apprentices around her. Each held a morning star in their hand and their task this morning was to see if one of them could score a direct hit on her. They'd been practicing for weeks and so far not one of them had.

Thirty minutes later with sweat pouring down her shirt Meredith understood why Mike had wanted to take the Almighty's name in vain. They seemed incapable of throwing the stars at her as a target, even when she stood immobile.

"I will take another try, Meredith," said Devon.

"You get to do it with me," said Gareth, stepping into the circle.

"I am capable of training them, Gareth."

He all but growled at her. "Meredith, you are done for today. I will take over."

"What if I insist?"

"But you will not. My way will inspire them. Go. Leave. Let me work this group the way it needs to be done."

There was something behind his rough smoky voice Meredith lately found mesmerizing.

"You seek to challenge me in this task?" he asked.

Meredith blinked. For a second she could have sworn his eyes had turned red. She must be overtaxing herself. "No. You are correct. I will leave them to your capable hands."

He nodded, another strange move which she found disconcerting.

"Thank you. I will ask another favor of you, Meredith. When I am done will you teach me more of your culture?"

Meredith smiled and her heart soared. "I would like that with my blessed heart."

"Great. I will come to you later tonight so my re-education can begin," said Gareth, moving back to the circle of would-be-angel soldiers.

"Okay, everyone. It's time you all learned hand-to-hand combat."

Meredith made her way over to the door. She heard Gareth remove his shirt and fought with herself not to turn around. He was a friend. That was all. Even after all she had offered, he continued to remain the perfect gentleman. His sense of honor demanded such but there were times when Meredith hated his morality and code of ethics. Ten years was a long time in exile and knowing her mate would never accept her often left her feeling isolated and alone. Lately, she wondered if this was the path of her life. With her heavenly heart she prayed to the Mistress for it not to be so.

Where Izzy fought the path Nathanael had set upon her, Meredith longed for it. A husband, confidant and more importantly, motherhood, had at one time been an integral part of her teachings. No longer. While her fellow Cherubs' future was often gifted to her, not once did the curse the Mistress leveled on her as penance, foretell anything but darkness for herself.

CHAPTER FOUR

M ike watched how Gareth finally got through to them. Brute punishment. When they didn't listen, he made them drop and give him twenty. If they hesitated he added ten more pushups. Now, he was waiting for Cole and Devon to try to tackle him. Mike found himself admiring the ex-soldier and it surprised him.

"When the demons come at you they will use everything in their arsenal. You must learn to think like one and move like one. Devon, you and Cole need to work more like a team. Cole if you come at my head, Devon you come at my feet. Tackle. And the only way to truly kill a demon is with holy water."

How does he know that?

Mike cleaned up the recreational center while Gareth gave out more instructions. When he urged them all to fight him, secretly Mike hoped his cocky self would get a beating. Sadly, that was not the case. The more Mike watched Gareth move, almost in a blur of fighting speed, his unease grew. When Gareth's right arm snapped back, twisting at a wrong angle, with him not flinching, Mike's gut twisted.

Two hours later training finished for the day.

"Gareth, where did you learn to fight like that?" asked Mike, casually moving a tumbler closer to Gareth's hand.

"Army," spat out Gareth.

"Really. I know a number of army guys and not one of them has your moves."

"Glad to hear it. Got any water behind the bar?"

"Sure, here you go," said Mike, pouring a large glass of water. Mike made sure when he handed it to Gareth he accidently spilled the tumbler. Gareth moved his fingers out of the liquid but not before Mike saw what he dreaded. Smoke.

Gareth looked at him, long and hard. It was on the tip of Mike's tongue to voice his crazy thoughts.

"You're getting clumsy, Mike."

"Sorry about that," said Mike. He'd wait until later to voice his fears to Izzy even if she thought he might be going insane. Then again a year ago, if anyone had told him angels and demons truly existed, he would have classified them as a nut job.

"Well, I've got to go. Someone around here has to make a decent living. Unlike you, we're not all filthy rich."

Now that sounded like Gareth.

"They say the richest person in the world is one who loves."

"Seriously, Mike get a hobby. You're becoming a romantic and it's not a nice trait. See you later," said Gareth.

Mike watched Gareth leave and felt his heart rate slow. Something these days felt wrong with Gareth. In walked Izzy and Nathanael, as Mike got ready to deal with the growing inventory he hadn't stocked.

"How did it go?" asked Izzy, sitting on the bar stool, looking regal but tired.

"I think the better question is how much did you curse?" asked Nathanael, with a laugh.

Mike grinned. "I'm trying not to curse but they don't make it easy. Listen, have you two noticed something odd lately with Gareth?" The minute he asked he wished he hadn't.

"He's trying to go clean and this is not an easy time for him," said Izzy.

Mike nodded but the unease he felt for Gareth did not fade.

"Is there more?" asked Nathanael, who looked the age of nineteen but had undertaken a lot to make the rank of Sera. The fact he didn't like to flaunt it spoke volumes. While Mike hadn't liked Nathanael in the beginning, he had started to admire Nathanael's strong, determined way. If anything, Mike respected his blunt demands which Izzy detested.

"Maybe...maybe not. He seemed to know things about killing demons I didn't think a guy in the army would know."

"Meredith has been helping Gareth and I am sure she has answered any questions he might have about demons. If there is one thing I know about Gareth it's that he likes to have lots of information when it comes to different situations and I would say learning the truth of our existence is that," said Izzy. "I will talk to Meredith to ease your mind. In the meantime, I would like to see this place you've secured for training."

Mike smiled. "Give me a minute to call my friend and I'll take you there."

"Trust me, Isabella, you will like it," said Nathanael.

"I am sure I will but I still would like to see it before we begin training. We can't have a place full of windows and we need to have privacy. Have you stressed such to your friend, Mike?"

Mike nodded. Izzy was nervous. She liked to be in control of everything but she'd allowed him and Nathanael to pick the training place.

A few minutes later they walked the four long blocks to the training center. It still amused Mike how much they hated being enclosed in vehicles. He'd have thought fast cars would have been right up an angel's alley. Sadly, it turned out only the earth-born angels had a true appreciation for luxury vehicles. Nathanael had stated quite plainly he didn't trust the metal cages and would rather walk any day than venture inside a beast of such nature. It had been on the tip of Mike's tongue to call him a scaredy-cat but he'd seen Nathanael's moves in action and knew first-hand the angel had deadly aim.

CHAPTER FIVE

Meredith walked into the common room and all the air left her. She knew that scent. Knew the angel deep in her soul who had somehow left the Heavens for Earth and was now standing next to the window. The spacious common room felt suffocatingly small and for an instant, Meredith thought to leave.

Then he turned. Aquamarine-colored eyes as light blue as the sky of her home zoned in on her. Meredith knew she should have fought with Izzy against Nathanael's plan.

"How fare thee?"

She was expected to answer. It was a question. He was Seraphim. Customs must be maintained. "I am fine."

He moved closer and it took a lot of willpower for Meredith not to move, not to scurry back a few steps or bow her head.

"I am sorry."

No, he's not. He had lectured enough to her and Izzy in the Heavens, telling them the consequences of their plan would only involve pain. He'd been correct.

"I had no idea the amount of time which had passed. You look the same."

He said it with such incredulous disbelief she wanted to believe him. Still, though Zachary, son to Gabriel, the Archangel, knew things about the Heavens which others did not. Meredith nodded, unsure how to respond. His Seraphim scent, all hot exotic male, made her feel dizzy and overly conscious she was wearing attire not befitting a Cherub. She'd been working out with the earth-born angels and was sweaty and tired.

"I take it you have agreed to help us," stated Meredith.

His eyebrows, those two dark arches she'd loved from the moment she'd spotted him, rose slightly. Meredith had changed. Her tone said it all.

"When Nathanael told me, I could not believe it. Earth-born angels against Lucifer's army. It will be a slaughter and foolish."

"Is that what you thought when you trained us?"

"You have changed, I see. Earth has made you more grounded. I am most pleased."

Meredith encroached on his space. Her anger rose swift and fast. "You knew training us would change us. Training these earth-born angels will reshape their destiny. Tell me Zachary, is that why you do it? Is that why you dared the wrath of your father to train us?"

Zachary's arms snagged Meredith's arms, pulling her in close. "You are angry. You and I both know why I trained you. Tell yourself different and you are telling a falsehood." The mere fact he'd broken protocol and had touched her spoke volumes, but she'd fooled herself once before with him and the consequences had been damning.

"Do you think it's been easy for me?" he asked, demanding she answer.

I do not want to care. I do not want to know. Meredith looked across the room, thinking so much had changed for her in a decade she didn't know where to begin. "It has been easier on you than on me."

"Not so." His voice dropped to that seductive low tone she loved.

"I am most honored Zachary that you will train them. We are undeserving of your skills." She kept her eyes downcast and pleaded with him to release her. His scent, leather and steel, his signature, threatened her control. It was always good to remind herself that when push came to shove, Zachary had turned away. He hadn't spoken one word in their defense when brought before the Septuagint Council or in private to his father.

He released her.

"I told you the consequences. Things though have changed in the Heavens since your exile."

For a second Meredith dared to hope that might mean something could exist between them. The second was very short-lived.

"I am bound to another."

He said it. He dared to speak what her heart had feared. The tears threatened to spring free, but with a steely will she held them at bay. At one time, the meek Meredith would have cried but not now. Not after everything she'd gone through. She'd wielded steel for reasons of vengeance, much like Izzy had and she would keep her promise.

Looking him squarely in the eyes, she said. "I am most pleased for you."

Then Meredith turned her back on Zachary and left the common room. She didn't flee to her own sanctuary, for that would allow her to wallow in self-pity and lots of what ifs. She trotted back down to the recreational center, pleased it was empty. This time when she took up her morning stars, she threw them with precision—dead-center on the dart boards. When that failed to appease her, she went behind the stage and took up her Kita and swung at her invisible opponent until sweat stained the front and back of her t-shirt.

"I think you have vanquished your foe," said Nathanael, startling Meredith. Her swing went wild and she had to pivot on the balls of her feet to keep her balance.

"Nathanael, you startled me."

"Sorry. I did make noise when I entered but you looked too engrossed to notice. Mind telling me what's up?"

"Nothing," replied Meredith, moving to place her sword back in its sacred place.

"That wouldn't have anything to do with Zach, would it?"

Always so perceptive. Zach. She tossed his nickname around in her mind, finding herself liking it a little too much. It was a strong, commanding name much like his full title.

"Nathanael, I am not sure how much Isabella has told you about our early days learning to fight, but I had thought not to encounter him again."

Nathanael approached her but carefully kept his distance. "I am most sorry to offend thee, Meredith and would not wish you anguish. I needed the best and Zach is such as you know. I only found out a few minutes ago the role he played in your exile. Had I known I would have asked another but it is done."

So, like a Seraphim. He'd stated his case, made his point and wanted her to accept it. Meredith nodded, but knew deep down she would not find this an easy time. "Does Isabella know he is here?"

"That is the reason we are back here. We had a quick tour of our new training facility but on the walk back as I told her the plans and how Zach was coming to assess the recruits, she dashed home cursing. I should warn you, she's in a foul mood."

I bet she is. After all, when the Council guards had come for them, she too had pleaded with Zachary to explain their reasons. At one time, Izzy had even said she'd like to kill that damn Sera. Meredith had known at the time she'd only voiced such anger because of his lack of action on their part.

Just then the door to the recreational center flew open and Izzy practically ran over to where they were.

"Oh, Meredith. I am so sorry. If I had known I'd never have agreed. Not that I agreed to your plan at all," said Izzy more to Nathanael than to her. "Nathanael will make him leave."

Nathanael moved toward Izzy. Whenever the two of them were together the need for them to touch was evident. Even though Izzy didn't want to fully tie herself to Nathanael, she had. Case in point, she actually leaned into his frame when he stepped to her side.

Nathanael spoke softly, "No Isabella, I will not ask him to leave. We need him."

"You cannot ask this of us," said Izzy, her eyes staying centered on Meredith.

It wasn't the us Izzy was referring to. It was for Meredith's sake. As much as Meredith loved her best friend, she knew in her heart Zachary's talent could help.

"Izzy, I am okay. Nathanael in this case is correct. You cannot train them. Zachary is needed and he will do his best."

"Like he did his best for us," said Izzy, with such hatred for a second Meredith wondered if she'd spoken aloud.

Those exact thoughts mirrored her own.

"It was different," said Nathanael.

"How so? He did not say one word in our defense," said Izzy.

Meredith had heard this argument enough to know there would be no winners. Wanting to end things, she spoke up. "Izzy, truly I am alright. You are worrying for naught. All will be okay. Zachary will help and we need him. And, were you not the person asking me to help you this morning with the earth-born angels? Why not let him take some of your burden?"

"Seriously, Meredith, sister of my heart, are you okay with him staying here?"

"Staying here?" blurted Meredith, praying and hoping she'd heard wrong.

"Why, yes. Mike has made room in the side office so Zachary could stay in the recreational center."

"In the center?" Meredith feared she was beginning to sound like a parrot. "Why can't he stay with Nathanael at the Seraphim Safe House?"

"Zach felt it best to stay close to the training center and it was all he asked," said Nathanael.

Meredith nodded but ground her teeth. She highly suspected there was more they'd agreed to but wouldn't press the point.

In walked Mike. "Everything okay?"

Nathanael nodded. "We're just working out the details of Zach's stay."

"The guy certainly travels light."

Meredith fought not to grin. She knew that first-hand. Possessions didn't adorn his heavenly room, unless it was a weapon. Those he had aplenty.

"Is there a problem here?"

Zach's voice slid loud yet soft through the center. Meredith fought not to run from the room. If anything, she knew she looked worse than she had an hour ago when she'd faced him down.

"No, Zach. There's no problem. Mike was pointing out you travel light," said Nathanael.

"Yes, and I was pointing out that it might be best for you to leave," said Izzy, with her hands on her hips.

Meredith gasped. She might think it but would never speak such, especially to him.

"You are the delight I recall. As usual not thinking but speaking."

If Nathanael hadn't grabbed Izzy's arm, Meredith was fairly certain Zach and Izzy would have had their first physical fight. In the Heavens they'd sparred both with words and weapons, usually with words first and then pointed swords.

"So, you two don't get along. That's just great," said Mike, running a hand over his weary looking face.

"They will get along fine. Won't you?" stated Nathanael to both Izzy and Zach.

Meredith knew it was the wrong question so she piped in. "They will. Now Izzy come with me while Nathanael shows Zachary what needs to be done." Meredith didn't wait for Izzy to speak. She grabbed her friend's arm and led her out.

Only when they were sequestered in the common room did Meredith feel the tension leave her body.

"You are not fooling me, Meredith. You can't like him being here."

No. I detest it. "We will make do. And he's helping."

Izzy harrumphed. "I sometimes wonder if his help got us kicked out of the Heavens."

"We asked him. Do not forget we approached him."

Izzy was rattled. She wouldn't sit on the sofa. She paced like a lioness along the length of the common room. "Not one word. He refused to help when we needed it most."

"No. There you are wrong. He told us squarely what he would and would not do for us when we negotiated terms for training." Remembering those days made Meredith's heart flutter.

"You can't be serious, Meredith. Things are not black and white and he knew it."

Meredith sat on the sofa, forcing a calm she didn't feel. "In the Heavens there is no gray. Zachary told us what he would and would not do. He told us plainly that if caught and brought before Council he would not stand up for us."

"But..."

"There is no but, Izzy. Zachary warned us."

"I do not regret the path I've chosen. Do you?"

Some days. Meredith looked at Izzy and as she stared into her friend's eyes she recalled that day long ago when they'd both lost their mothers thanks to the demon attack on the Heavens. She stood up and took Izzy's hands in her own.

"Never. This is our path. I never want to be helpless again and thanks to Zachary we are not." I can't believe I'm defending him.

"But...he...he broke your heart."

So that's why Izzy is truly riled. "Oh, Izzy. I knew the minute I asked him to train us what would happen."

"But, it's not fair to you."

"Heavenly law is never fair but we must move on. I have forgiven him." Not really, but there is no point in dwelling in the past.

"Nat said he is bound to another."

"You knew we were bound together?" This news rattled Meredith. She had not spoken, even to her BFF, of their pre-ordained ties.

Izzy reached out and grasped Meredith's hands. "He told me the first day I approached him to train us."

This Meredith had not known.

"He also said if he trained you, the arrangement would be terminated by his father."

Meredith felt tears gather and had to blink. "Why did you not tell me?"

"We needed to learn to fight. It was the lesser of the two evils. But Meredith, I gambled your future and happiness and I was wrong to not tell you all the facts," said Izzy, forcing Meredith and her to the sofa.

Meredith reclaimed her hands. "I knew the gamble. I have no regrets."

Izzy gave a small smile. "Yes, you do. Even I have regrets. If you are truly okay with him being here, I will refrain from killing him," said Izzy, a smile lighting up her face.

Meredith highly suspected the notion of killing Zachary thrilled her more than what mattered to her.

"He can help us," said Meredith.

"Sometimes I wonder if Zachary only helps himself," said Izzy, jumping up to leave the room.

Sad, Izzy had spoken the very words rattling around in Meredith's head. No taint dared to stain Zachary's family lineage; after all he came from a line of perfect angels.

Meredith sighed. Coming to Earth she'd learned a hard lesson. Like humans, no angels were perfect.

CHAPTER SIX

After two days of re-learning Cherub culture, Ash masquerading as Gareth couldn't stomach another lesson.

"Would you like to learn more about defending yourself from a demon?" asked Meredith.

"I think I know all that is required," answered Ash, trying not to wince. What little the Cherubs knew of demons he found truly enlightening. "I think the time has come for us to put the earth-born angels to the test."

"I couldn't agree with you more," said Izzy, walking into the library. Her Kita hung deceptively at her side but Ash had seen her in action and knew the skill with which she wielded the sword.

"Well, in this we agree. You lead the way, Izzy and I will round up the willing victims," said Ash as he maneuvered around Meredith and Izzy.

Meredith gave him one of her looks. "You really shouldn't call them victims. They are trying to be helpful."

"Helpful won't help against a demon army," said Ash. "Give me ten minutes I will meet you both outside."

They nodded and Ash finally escaped. Time stretched before him. The temptation to visit Shea's room overwhelmed him. He sobered his thoughts. Regaining control of his emotions he pivoted and fled down the stairs to the recreational center where he found his victims. What Izzy had in mind for them mystified him but if they were to succeed against his father's army, they first had to learn what they were up against.

Winter's eyes looked large and scared in the dark alley and Ash fought not to groan. With Meredith, Izzy, Nathanael and the six earth-born angels clustered around the alley they were using for training, they were like a flare to any demons in the area.

Izzy stepped out of the crowd. "Draw your weapons and be prepared. They will come at you with strength that will surprise you. All of you have your vials of holy water and all of you have dipped your morning stars, right?"

They all nodded. Ash stepped more into the shadow of the alley. A streetlight gave off a flickering beacon but it wasn't much illumination. Demons didn't need the light to see. Darkness was their home.

Izzy drew her short knife out of her belt loop and quicker than he anticipated she slashed at her palm. Ash gasped. Angel blood. Its power and essence beckoned to the demon he was and his head buzzed with the pull. Thankfully the power of Izzy's blood also brought forth the demons Ash had sensed in the area and within minutes they were all fighting. Ash easily jumped into the fray, kicking and maiming when he could but truthfully this fight wasn't about him. This fight was a test for the earth-born angels and while they seemed to be holding their own, their lack of skill became truly evident.

Cole clipped a demon with his morning star and Devon finished another demon off. The two worked like pros, diving into the battle with a ferociousness Ash liked. These two knew how to fight when it counted. Sky moved easily, her slight frame making it easy for her to duck blows from the two demons coming at her and Winter used a sword like it was an extension of her arm, which shocked Ash. But while Sky could move fast, she hadn't made one kill and Winter's skill with the sword, while good, wasn't enough. When a fifth demon moved from the darkness Ash stepped forward aiming to kill the demon but within seconds he stilled.

It can't be her.

"Do I render you speechless, brother? Even wearing that human disguise, I could smell you anywhere."

Ash had the sense to look around, relieved to notice with the melee no one could hear her.

"You are not real. You are dead."

She laughed. The sound was as rich and unfettered as he recalled from his childhood. There before him stood his sister, Kali.

"I, my brother dear, am alive but you are about to be turned to ash." Kali raised her sword and Ash was too stunned to move. Winter barreled her way between him and his sister. It was Winter who felt the full brute force of his sister's sword and only at the last minute did Ash push her out of the way, attempting to spare the Earth-angel.

Kali laughed again. Some things hadn't changed. Whenever they'd battled, she'd laughed crazily with glee. Ash raised his sword and they dueled like they had as children, each vying for a victory while hoping to catch their father's approval. Time stood still and Ash's body recalled all his sister's tricks. Her feet swept out and he easily jumped to avoid them. He flipped his sword to his left hand to block her assault.

More than anything Ash had questions roaring in his head. His father had killed Kali right before his eyes to show him what happened to those who failed him. Ash was fairly certain he'd gone mad after that because he'd been put in a hole for five years after that eventful day which had been etched in his memory like Hell fire.

Ash felt more than saw Izzy head his way. "You need to leave."

"Not before I have your head," replied his sister.

"I have no idea how you're alive. I saw father kill you. This is not what you think. I will come to you, but you must go. They have dipped their weapons in holy water."

Kali pivoted on her feet and Ash used the advantage to grab her arm, making it look like his sword would end her life. "I will explain," he whispered and then begged, "Now disappear."

"This is not over," said Kali as she finally did as instructed.

Breathing easy, Ash finally turned his attention to Winter. Meredith knelt at her side, while attempting to staunch Winter's gash.

"Izzy we've got to get her back to the house," said Meredith.

Izzy, Cole and Devon along with Nathanael quickly finished off the rest of the demons in the alley and all of them ran toward Winter. Ash picked up Winter and stepped from the alley with her in his arms. He highly suspected Kali's sword had been heated with hellfire, which would make healing Winter almost impossible, but he daren't speak his knowledge. His gut told him his sister was out for his blood. Vengeance was part of their shared history.

Nathanael jogged beside him as they all made their way back to the brownstone. There standing on the doorstep the last angel he expected to see, Shea. She stood, regal and beautiful with her long ebony hair cascading wildly down her back. He smiled. She blended so easily with the night his heart sped up.

"What happened?"

"We were training with demons and she got hurt," answered Meredith.

"Demons?" asked Shea, backing up, stepping into the hall's shadows.

"Gareth, take Winter upstairs to the bedroom next to mine," ordered Meredith. Ash didn't want to do as instructed but had no choice. He passed Shea without a word and truly the act almost killed him.

"It's okay Shea. The demons won't come here. This was a training exercise," said Meredith.

"Will she live?" asked Shea.

Meredith's voice floated softly up the stairs and Ash thanked his heightened demon hearing.

"I'm not sure. She's very hot. Almost feverish and I wouldn't have expected that from a sword gash. I'm wondering if there's more at play here. Will you help?"

"Oh...I...yes of course," said Shea and for once Ash was pleased with his enhanced demon hearing.

CHAPTER SEVEN

S hea clutched the curtain with her right hand. She had moved into the bedroom with the sick earth-born angel for reasons she couldn't understand. She had of course waited for Meredith to settle her and it wasn't until the entire household was lost in their dreams that Shea dared to venture from her upstairs room to the lower level where Winter rested on the bed. The scent of death hung like the rising aroma of fresh bread, heavy in the air and thick on her tongue. Shea hated how much the scent clung like a perfume to her skin. Darkness had eased into the night. The type of dark Shea had started to love a little too much. At two in the morning this was the darkness she liked best–it felt soft yet sinister at the same time and it empowered a person to think of illicit passions.

Edging away from the safety of the curtain, Shea made her way to Winter's side. For hours they'd sung to her in the hopes their powerful voices would heal the young woman. Shea had known it wouldn't work but she'd kept her knowledge snug to herself. Singing with her sisters used to comfort her, but it had the reverse effect today. She had been the outcast and chanting with her sisters had only reminded her how much had changed in so little time.

Picking up Winter's overly warm hand she knelt beside her bed. For a moment she thought to pray but the words choked her throat and it felt so sacrilegious to her soul she faltered. Instead, she tucked Winter's hand back under the blanket and stood. She'd wanted to hum an old song earlier but hadn't mustered the nerve to mention it to her fellow sisters. Now, though the room was empty and Shea would sing.

Lowering her head, she let the heat of the hum work her throat and then ever so softly she let the music pass through her almost closed lips. Time slipped from her mind, but that did not mean she did not feel, more than hear Ash's presence fill the small bedroom. Always at this hour he sought her out.

"You cannot save her."

His voice caused goosebumps to rise all over her body. Shea tried as usual to tell her body not to respond but like most things lately, her body didn't listen to her wishes. Ash didn't speak for several minutes. Rather he blended in with the ebony-hues of the room and it wasn't until those strong invisible arms of his wrapped around her middle that Shea realized how much his mere touch warmed all of her.

"I thought to try," she said.

"That hymn you were humming, I recognize it."

"You do?"

He laughed. The sensation of his soft, vibrant voice and chest rattling laughter sounded eerily loud in the room. "I am not ignorant. My education was vast and that hymn if I recall is known as the Waking Dead."

Shea nodded, trying with all her might not to lean into his embrace.

"I will not think less of you if you lean onto me, Shea."

Not my b'iã. If he'd named her, she'd stiffen and shrug out of his hold. In lieu of such she found herself yearning for what he offered; not good. He had been the one to make her crave the dark and he was the one who now made her like the scent of death. Shea mentally made a note to make a long list of whys she should never give into Ash's warmth.

"She's been poisoned with hellfire," said Ash.

"Then she will die."

"No. She will turn into a shade, which is much worse," said Ash, letting his head nuzzle the top of her head.

"Why tell me this?"

"I thought you might want to know."

She did. But this conversation, the normality of it, scared her.

"My search continues but I am making progress."

Shea turned into his embrace at those word. Progress. Her heart sped up. Hope for the first time flew threw her.

"I believe she is being kept in a place called The Precipice."

It was not a word Shea knew. Nor did she want to fully understand what it was. All she cared about was a place had been discovered and her twin might be there. Armed now with a word, she would do what must be done.

Winter moaned, causing Shea to slip from Ash's hold. "How long before she becomes a shade?"

"At best guess two days."

"Then I will leave you to your appointed task and I will inform Izzy."

Ash pulled her back to him. This was a first. He was usually very gentle when touching her but this move told her how much more he offered. Shea had to fight the shiver of desire skidding through her body and consciousness. Him being gentle, she could handle. Ash being demanding as the right of a Seraphim was a sight to behold.

"Telling her would not benefit either of you. There is nothing Izzy can do for the earth-born angel. She would question where your newfound knowledge came from."

Izzy would do that, but Shea knew she would not remain silent. A telling of a lie was impossible for an angel whereas omission was a learned skill. The fact Ash worried about her safety made a part of her smile. With care she controlled her facial features. Letting him know she liked his worry was not something she dared to admit.

"That may be but I will inform her of what I know. You can trust me not to mention you."

Shea was fairly certain Ash was smiling as he said, "Oh, please do tell her it came from me. She'd be overcome with joy hearing my name."

Shea couldn't stop the smile this time. This side of him, caring and witty, charmed her.

Not good. Not good at all.

"Might I suggest you tell her you recall reading of such. I am not comfortable placing you in a questioning light with your fellow sisters," said Ash.

His notion held merit. "That I can arrange."

"I must go while darkness lingers but I find it harder and harder to leave you."

His admission caused her heart to flutter and Shea felt sure he knew.

"You promised to find her. Use your time wisely," admonished Shea.

He nuzzled the top of her head. It was an action he liked to do and one she had started to appreciate.

"I love your hair," he said.

She fought not to laugh. "You are stalling. Go. Do what I have asked."

This time he kissed the top of her head.

"I will always do what you ask," he said and then a second later the cold of the room was her sole companion.

CHAPTER EIGHT

S hea had poked her head in Izzy's room at the beginning of dawn. She had been timid but her disclosure Winter would turn into a shade in less than forty-eight hours made Izzy's heart ache. She wasn't sure how Shea had reasoned such but the truth of her discovery had felt like a sword had pierced Izzy's heart. After thanking Shea for her insight, Izzy sat on the bed feeling overwhelmed. Part of that had to do with the weariness she felt of late for the tasks the Mistress kept appointing to them, and her struggle to maintain her "dating" relationship with Nathanael.

She felt pulled in many directions and not one gave relief. She knew the type of ecstasy Nathanael offered but giving into her destiny, and one taste of what he offered; she'd be lost. She knew it wasn't fair to play him along but losing herself in what he had to offer she couldn't accept. Especially not while trying to fight off demons about to lay siege to the Heavens and she would never leave her fellow fallen sisters to the plight of Earth on their own.

The bigger question was how Shea knew what would happen to Winter. When pressed though Shea had closed up and Izzy hadn't wanted to push the still-broken angel. So much had happened to them all, but Shea had been the most brutally betrayed and it wasn't within Izzy to demand more of her. Maybe at one time she'd been a stronger leader and would have forced answers without care for the consequences. Lately, she wondered if that "caring" notion got in the way of her doing her job.

Feeling a need to harden herself, Izzy marched up to the elegant ultra-modern building and without further ado rang the bell. She would rather be fighting demons than standing on the stoop of the earth-born Cherub safe house but she needed help. Zachary, the one angel she loathed as much as Meredith, had informed her that the Doyen of the house might have the knowledge she sought to help Winter. She had scoffed at the idea but to ignore it meant Winter would turn into a shade and another guilt trip was something Izzy didn't need. The fact that Zachary seemed to know something of the workings of the earth-born Cherubs startled Izzy. Already guilt weighed her down with thoughts she'd gotten Winter into this mess. The earth-born angels, while willing pupils, couldn't hold off an army. The realization they needed more, and most importantly angel warriors who knew how to wield weapons with deadly aim, had become her newfound prayer.

The door opened. Izzy was astonished the Doyen herself answered.

"With honor, please enter our sanctuary. Our house is your house by the blessed light."

The words spoken in English were the customary greeting any Cherub angel would give to another seeking to enter their house. For a moment, Izzy wondered if the Doyen could speak Scripture.

Izzy bowed her head as was custom and answered. "My heart is warmed by your offer and I accept the blessing of the light." She walked past the Doyen and waited for the door to shut before letting her lead the way to the office.

But it wasn't the Doyen's office they went to. They entered the prayer room. Izzy knew this because she and her fellow fallen angels had stayed one week with the Doyen in the beginning. They had thought they could fit in, only to quickly discover their differences set them apart too much to be fully welcomed. The prayer room, with its floor to ceiling windows, let the warmth of the sun stream through. The only thing in the room was the blessed holy water held in an antique crudely-fashioned brown basin on a pine wooden dais. It had been the one room to comfort Izzy when she'd needed to heal. Izzy hadn't prayed then. Her anger at what had befallen her fellow sisters hadn't allowed her the meditation of prayer and Izzy knew it was the warmth of the sun which had eased her heart more than the recitation of prayer.

The Doyen looked the same. Her silver hair was held back in its usual severe bun, and as was customary she wore a striped-business suit cut below the knees. A white dress shirt was fully buttoned up to her neck. By comparison, Izzy, who had decided to wear the traditional jeans and black shirt she'd started to get accustomed to, felt underdressed.

"I'm sure you heard what happened to Winter," said Izzy, stepping into the prayer room.

"I had heard. How is she doing?"

"Not great. Turns out she's been poisoned by hellfire."

The Doyen stopped in her approach to the basin of water. She pivoted and turned. "Are you sure?"

Izzy moved closer to the Doyen. Truthfully, she wanted to watch the Doyen's expression. While the Cherub safe house had been welcoming, she'd always felt there were secrets within the walls of the house and she highly suspected it was the Doyen who controlled everything in the sanctuary. "We are fairly certain."

"Hellfire poison is quite rare. Only the highest of demons would have access to that poison."

Well, that information was new. The only high-ranking demon she knew was Ash but she hadn't seen him in weeks, thanks be to the blessed light.

"And it is usually only used on another demon."

"What?" asked Izzy, her mind skidding to a halt with the Doyen's words.

"Hellfire poison is a tool used by demons to control another demon."

Izzy tried to recall who was with Winter when she had been attacked. Gareth had been the first to respond but the other earth-born Seraphims had also been close to Winter.

"Would you have the antidote?" asked Izzy. That had been the sole reason she'd ventured to the house in the first place.

"There is no antidote. The only way to save Winter from turning into a shade is to let a demon absorb her blood and then give her a transfusion."

And that's so easy. Izzy almost laughed. Letting a demon absorb her blood gave a demon a lot of power and in doing so they would likely kill Winter. Nice quick fix, she thought.

"It can be done," said the Doyen, letting her pale blue eyes rest on Izzy.

"Can it be done successfully? I'm not keen on letting a demon come into its full powers knowing full well it could as easily kill Winter."

"If you capture a demon in a holy circle they can't escape. The trick is knowing when to kill the demon without leaving a taint of the poison within Winter. All it takes is one drop of hellfire left in her system to kill her."

"You can't be serious. A holy circle? A demon would know what was happening when the circle was drawn and the candles lit."

"Yes, but sometimes the euphoria of human blood or in this case angel blood overweighs common sense for demons."

Izzy watched as the Doyen placed the tips of her fingers in the blessed holy water. While the Doyen bowed her head in prayer Izzy made a startling realization."

"What, you are saying this has been done before?" she asked.

The Doyen removed her fingers from the holy water and knelt on the wooden floor. Comfort like in Heaven didn't equate with prayer and the need for humility.

"Yes."

"Did the person live?" asked Izzy, her mind trying to figure out the plausibility of all of it.

"I did."

Those two words moved Izzy so much she found herself kneeling beside the Doyen. "Why didn't you tell me?"

"You never asked."

"You must have known I was going out nightly to fight the demons. Why didn't you say something?"

"What would you have me say? You walked into our sanctuary with judgment clearly evident in your eyes. It was not my duty to show you the way. Our history is as different as yours. I tried in the beginning to inform you but you didn't want the truth."

"The truth?"

"Not all of us use swords or Kitas as our weapons. We are earth-born angels. Did you never question our existence?"

"I know little of it," admitted Izzy, feeling for the first time she might have misjudged the Doyen.

"We have an entire library detailing how we came to exist and our Earth-bound purpose. While we serve the Almighty in every way, we serve another first."

This news startled Izzy. Loyalty to another was a sacrilegious thought. "And who would that be?"

The Doyen stood up and stepped back from Izzy. "Our creator–Lilith, we have granted first allegiance to as our sacred oath."

Izzy felt the world she knew tilt. Lilith? What little she'd gleamed of Lilith jumped into her mind and honestly none of it made sense.

"I see the news of Lilith upsets you. I am not sure of your heavenly teachings but how did you think we came into existence?"

Izzy swallowed. "In truth, I never gave it thought. I thought you were all humans who wanted to honor the Almighty."

The Doyen cracked a smile and for the first time Izzy saw a hint of vulnerability behind the Doyen's beautifully crafted made-up face. "We are earth-born angels but to be so we all had to die first. Each of us has been to the cross-roads and each of us was asked by Lilith if we wanted to return to Earth with the understanding we could make amends for our faults."

"Faults?" Izzy felt stunned and more than slightly stupid for not knowing the earth-born angels' origin.

"Every one of us committed grievous crimes while on Earth and Lilith offered us redemption. Once we accepted, we changed."

Izzy couldn't fathom what type of crimes Winter, Sky or the others had undertaken since they seemed so young. "Changed?"

The Doyen nodded and then led the way from the prayer room to another room further down the hall. When Izzy stepped inside, she knew it was a library of sorts. Large ancient looking books lined the multitude of shelves. Some looked to be falling apart. A few were precious enough to be placed under the protection of glass. The Doyen softly closed the door.

"How old do you think I am?" asked the Doyen.

Izzy blurted out what she thought. "Thirty something."

A sad look flitted across the Doyen's face. "I am two hundred and thirty-seven. When I accepted Lilith's offer, even I didn't understand the consequences, but I would not change my fate. Like you, Izzy, we are frozen in time."

Izzy's legs felt wooden. She somehow reached the brown leather sofa lining the wall and slumped into it.

"But why?"

"It is Lilith's way. There's more."

"More than this, wonderful news."

"Lilith's change made a part of us demon. We all strive to tamp that aspect down and that's part of our daily fight and reason why it's hard for us to fight demons. Some of us over the years have not fought that fight with honor and have become fully fledged demons. My task as Doyen has been to ensure the women under my care do not turn."

A gasp flew from Izzy and she quickly rose to her feet. "That's not true. You don't smell like a demon."

The Doyen laughed. Izzy didn't think the subject matter was light-hearted at all and nothing about this discovery did she find remotely amusing.

"Why thank you. I would never want to smell like a demon. Every time we fight them, and we do, we feel a powerful pull to that dark side. Lilith warned us this would happen when we transformed. We must always fight that stain and pull to the dark side. For those of us, lucky enough to get our wings, they are not white like yours, rather black with white tips.

"But black wings are for demons," stated Izzy, trying to sort out this newfound knowledge.

"I think the white tips are actually quite pretty, don't you?" said the Doyen, stepping back and letting her wings show.

Izzy felt longing deep within her gut. She forced herself to look more closely at the Doyen and had to admit the black wings with white tips were stunning.

"So how did you achieve your wings?" asked Izzy.

"I agreed to become Doyen and lead the next group of women into the fight and I saved a human soul. A human soul who was quite important," she added, and in a blink her wings disappeared.

Something deep within Izzy's heart ached. She ignored it. She'd given up her wings when offered by the Mistress. Accepting them after the heavenly Council had brutally hacked them off would have meant leaving her fellow fallen Cherub sisters. That was something she would never do. "But why would Lilith oversee this?"

"That I can't answer. But I will certainly help you find a way to heal Winter."

Izzy found herself pacing the small room. "But you let me believe you were all helpless. More interested in fashion and accessories and your fast cars than demon hunting."

"I never told you otherwise."

There was that damn angel omission art in full form. Izzy knew she was pacing the room, feeling slightly cornered.

She felt another whirlwind of emotions. "Are you prepared to fight demons?"

The Doyen stood. "We have been preparing since the beginning of our existence. While our ways might not be as direct as yours, we are tasked with helping humans who become stained with darkness to find the path of light. It's the only way we can get our wings."

"I think Doyen you and I should have a candid talk and I think it best we invite another to join us."

"Another?" There was clear surprise in the Doyen's voice.

"Yes another. The Mistress."

The Doyen immediately fell to her knees to prostrate herself. "We would be most honored for a visit and deep within my heart I will admit I've longed for such."

Really. She's not all that she's cracked up to be. Izzy refrained from speaking what she thought. The Mistress and her, had a not-so-friendly relationship, but Izzy knew the only way to move things forward was to do something she hated–pray.

CHAPTER NINE

Meredith wanted to fight in solitude but Zachary would have none of it. When she'd first entered the new gym with her Kita she'd been pleased to find it empty. That emptiness had lasted the all of about ten minutes. In had walked Zachary, hoisting a large duffel bag over his shoulder looking so Seraphim but equally so manly, she'd almost hidden behind a large pillar. That wouldn't have been very Cherub of her so she'd continued with her warm-up, never expecting him to dump the bag and quickly remove his own sword so he could spar with her.

Thirty minutes later with sweat running down her back and front, they still hadn't spoken.

"You are favoring your left arm to block. Don't."

She'd give him don't. Switching hands faster than he could blink she attacked, pleased for a mere second to see his astonished face. She pushed forward wanting to inflict damage, knowing she couldn't. When her Kita nicked his right cheek and a trickle of his golden-hued blood streaked across his too-perfect face she stumbled, fell to her knees and reverently bowed her head to apologize.

She didn't expect Zachary to laugh. He'd never laughed at home. His deep baritone voice, both exotic and sinful, Meredith fought to ignore. She realized it was a good thing he hadn't laughed in the Heavens when he'd trained them because she might have given into her destiny then, and where would she be now? She found herself giving into a silent chuckle with the absurdity of it all. She'd given him up the moment she'd agreed with Izzy to take up arms and she was the one who had to accept things.

"I have obviously underestimated your improved skills, Meredith."

Her head flew up. He's spoken her name. She tried to recall if he'd ever done that before and couldn't. The sight of the gold-hued blood steadily dripping down his check actually pleased her. She, Meredith, one of the cursed fallen angels had marred the Almighty angel Zachary. If only that could be recorded in one of the heavenly scribes.

He extended a hand to her to help her up. Will wonders never cease, thought Meredith. Ignoring his offer, she stood on her own two feet. After all, she'd been doing nothing less for well over a decade thanks to being kicked out of her home.

Their moment ended when the rest of the group, including the earth-born Seraphim angels, stormed through the door. Gareth lagged behind but it was he who first noticed the scratch on Zachary's face.

"Looks like Meredith scored a direct hit on you, Zachary." Gareth's voice was full of mockery and for a second she wondered what Zachary would say and do.

"That she has. But alas, I only allow one scratch a day so my quota is all used up. Grab your weapons and let's begin." He dismissed her by simply turning from her to walk back to his duffel bag to pull out an even bigger sword. Momentarily, Meredith wondered what other hidden weapons rested in his bag.

Meredith swiped her sweaty hair off her forehead and put her weapons away. She'd scored her victory of the day and would savor it–or maybe the sound of Zachary's laughter more.

"I will leave you to train them," said Meredith.

"I was hoping you'd spend more time with the girl and help her throw stars properly."

Meredith looked at Zachary. He was asking for her help. Will the Heavens flood? "Sure, that makes sense." It didn't but she wasn't in the mood to spare more with Zachary whether with words or weapons.

Meredith reached for her Kita she'd laid on the floor. Her blanket of hair fell over her face.

"Tie your hair back to keep it from hindering your movements," ordered Zachary.

Yes, that was the voice she was used to. Commanding, while sounding slightly annoyed he had to deal with females.

Meredith gave a mocking bow and with skill flipped her Kita to her back and within seconds had her long hair knotted and secured in place. "More to your liking?"

Zachary barely glanced her way. "This is not a game. Take training serious and you might succeed in this quest."

What was unspoken was they hadn't succeeded in their first quest–equality. While Zachary's speech was directed at the group, Meredith knew it was directed at her. Okay, so much for him being playful. That mood had obviously dissipated like a snuffed candle.

With burning anger surging forward, she marched over to the side of the room. Sky followed her. She asked how Winter was doing. Worry creased her forehead, making her look older than her seventeen years. Meredith told her there was no change. Meredith also prayed Izzy would have some helpful knowledge when she returned from her quest to visit the Doyen.

"When you throw a star, they are expecting you to aim for their heart. Don't. Aim for their throat or their eyes. A morning star thrown correctly will tear open an artery. A morning star dipped in holy water will kill a demon. It's best to keep the stars on a belt wrapped around your middle with the stars strapped to the front of the belt for easy access."

Meredith proceeded to show her how best to throw with a flick of her wrist. Two hours later, Meredith's wrist felt like it was on fire. Sky had to leave to attend university classes.

"I thought you were in high school," said Meredith.

"I skipped two grades. I'm in my first year at Boston U. I will return after classes."

"Please, join us after prayers, you are more than welcome to join Anya tonight. She's teaching her first religious class and is nervous so your presence would be welcome."

"What is she teaching?"

Sky was the curious one. Winter was the daring one, who was hurt and barely breathing. Sad, Meredith had labeled them such.

"The story of Lilith," said Meredith, tucking her stars back in place on her belt, but not before she caught a guarded look from Sky.

"I will pass tonight because of school work. See you tomorrow," she said.

Meredith nodded. She yearned for a cup of coffee and inwardly laughed. She was becoming addicted to the earthly brew as much as the teens who crowded in queues at coffee shops. She didn't want to turn her attention to the grunts coming from the other side of the room. She yearned not to look, but her eyes were traitorous. They sought out what her body desired but what her heart knew could never be hers. Zachary and Gareth had removed their shirts and were blocking blows. They looked evenly matched when in truth that shouldn't be the case. Zachary was a full-fledged Seraphim warrior. He had hundreds of years of experience. Gareth, while military trained, shouldn't be able to hold his own against an angel. But he was. When he flipped Zachary to his back and slid the sword he was holding to his neck, Meredith wanted to clap. She barely refrained. How unbecoming an angel, she had become. That didn't stop a small smile from escaping.

With her breath in her throat, she waited for two heartbeats before Gareth eased the blade from Zachary's neck and held out his hand.

Zachary jumped to his feet, unassisted. The last thing he'd ever do is reach for that helping hand, thought Meredith.

The two men put aside their weapons and wiped their faces with their shirts. Gareth gave her a wink when she walked over.

"Seems I've managed to impress Zachy here," said Gareth.

Zachy? The name fit a three-year-old, not a Seraphim warrior and certainly not one annoyed Zachary, who looked like he was barely restraining wiping his sword clean and not cleaving off Gareth's head.

"You must be famished. Join us for a meal," said Meredith.

Zachary gave her a curt nod and Gareth casually draped an arm around her shoulder. She should shrug out of his hold. That's what Zachary expected. Meredith smiled.

"What say you Zachy? Food it is. They Nayla a feast here," said Gareth, egging him on.

Zachary finished zipping up the duffel bag. "I would be honored to share a meal but first I must cleanse."

"Cleanse?" asked Gareth, giving a sniff to his armpit.

Meredith elbowed him.

"Think Zachy's got a point. I'll shower and then join you."

Meredith nodded. Showering wasn't exactly what Zachy had in mind but she wasn't about to disclose his true purpose. Praying, she highly suspected, wasn't viewed as a manly occupation.

She watched Gareth grab his stuff and give a fake salute as he exited the building.

"What do you know of that human?" asked Zachary.

No way would she be able to refer to him as Zachy with that baritone voice. "He's a good man with his own demons."

Zachary didn't say anything else. He simply picked up his mountain of a duffel bag and strode out of the building. That was his way. To Hell with asking how her training went or her bloody day. Meredith felt a blooming headache begin and knew he was her ailment. He would be her tormentor for days on end. All because she dared to follow her heart and not her pre-ordained duty.

CHAPTER TEN

A sh wanted to rip Zachary's head off. He'd known the minute he'd walked into the training room who that damn angel was. Zachary, the legendary Seraphim warrior who was said to have single-handily taken down a hundred soldiers belonging to his father's realm. While that might have impressed him, the demon within him had sought to show him who was boss. Luckily, Shea had reached out to touch his thoughts. He'd stumbled when he'd first felt her tentative touch. She had never reached out to him before and while he'd known her capable of such, her move, a step forward for their relationship, had shocked him. So much so, Zachary had scored a direct hit to his shoulder and right leg, forcing him to the ground. That touch though had enabled Ash to realize he had to get control. His task was bigger than killing Zachary, even though it would give him great delight, but it would not make it right. Might make my day but that's not my end goal.

Ash was going out of his freaking mind. Of course, the one night he'd attended a religious meeting and who was the bloody topic–Lilith. Demon bloods! His father, thank hellfire, couldn't see him, or he would have had an embolism. Ash almost grinned. He'd kill a thousand of his sire's legions to see Lucifer bleed. And if anything could make his father hurt it was Lilith. He knew more about Lilith, bitch that she was, than he could ever disclose. Lilith was the reason he had a half-sister. For over a millennium she'd been his father's Mistress, the one true Queen of Hell. Cold-hearted did not aptly describe her. Not once had she shown him an ounce of kindness. Floggings by her lovely hands did not count.

Ash kept his mouth shut. Thank the scribes no earth-born angels had shown up for the meeting. Honestly, he couldn't stomach another minute with them. He'd had enough of them for one day and if Zachy dared pretend to be interested in this crap, Ash felt certain he would not be able to contain his true self. As it was, holding onto Gareth's form was becoming more complicated. Who knew the human soldier was such a staunch fighter? Kudos to him but if he didn't simmer down with his constant screaming in Ash's head, he would kill him. Would frying his brain hurt? He might not be able to speak but maybe that tradeoff wouldn't be so bad.

Over an hour later he was finally alone with Anya. Shy, quiet as a newly lit candle, this young girl had been thrown to the wolves of mankind. He wondered how by the Heavens had Isabella been able to recruit the nun-like novice to dare take up arms in the heavenly war. She had a secret he'd ached to discern but more than that she had information he needed tonight–not tomorrow.

"Anya, that was a lovely talk," lied Ash. "I am wondering if you've ever heard of The Precipice?"

"Why?"

Interesting. She didn't say no, simply why. She knew something. Clever little thing.

"Just wondered. Someone mentioned something about a place in-between the heavenly realm and Earth," said Ash, running a hand through his hair as he leaned a hip on the desk. He tried to look relaxed but the idea of flirting with Anya recoiled him. Now flirting with Shea, who was upstairs, supposedly suffering a headache as her sisters had disclosed for her reason not to attend the religious class, stirred every aspect of him.

"Who said that?" Anya asked, pretending to not notice him as she restacked her books and journals.

"Can't remember. Think it was one of the Earth-angels. I thought it weird."

"We don't talk about it."

"Oh, why?" asked Ash, casually moving from the desk to scoop up her stacked books so he could ensure she didn't bolt for the door.

"It's a stain."

So, earnest she stated such, Ash almost laughed. Stains. Sins. Evil. That most certainly didn't happen in the heavenly realm. The mockery of it all sickened Ash.

"Can't have stains in the Heavens," said Ash, mockingly. No way could he say that with a straight face.

Anya eyed the door. "I should be on my way."

"Of course. Sorry, I'm taking up your time. I'll carry these for you back to your room."

Anya looked at the floor. Not a speck of dirt or dust dare to mar these floors but she looked at the worn wooden floor like it could see into her soul. Her cheeks were splotchy red with embarrassment. "Thank you, but no. I'm good."

She held out her hands, waiting for him to gently deposit the books into her arms.

Ash needed answers. "If I was interested in learning more about Lilith (Ash almost gagged saying her name aloud) and this so-called stain, because Anya I am truly intrigued and I love a good mystery, would you be able to point me in the right direction?"

Ash placed the books into her arms.

"I'm not sure I should," she said, shifting the weight of the books more to her left arm.

"I promise not to pester you. I'm simply curious."

Anya gave him a long hard look. She bit her lower lip, making her look even younger than her seventeen years.

"There is one book which might have some information," she said, so quietly Ash had to lean closer to discern her words.

"A book? What's it called." And more importantly how do I get my hands on it.

"Let me think on this. I need to do a bit of research first. I'm not sure the book I'm thinking of is it so give me a few nights."

Nights? Days? She was out of her freaking mind. Time was ticking and his enemy edged closer. Ash didn't have time to wait. Ash didn't like what he was about to do but the greater good for his b'iã had to be served. He glanced at the door; still shut. He used his powers to lock it.

"What are you doing?" asked Anya.

Ash turned his face to her, knowing his eyes glowed red. "I need information you are keeping in your precious head and I don't have time to wait."

Anya gasped and attempted to move. Ash grasped her face and held it between his hands. The books dropped loudly to the floor. He prayed no one came barreling in because of the noise. Using his powers, he sifted through her brain, knowing it would cost her. Tucked neatly away in a far corner of her mind, almost closed off from her awareness, he found what he sought. The book called Acclamations of Dissent, was actually hidden within another book. That made perfect sense to Ash. Heavenly sins and secrets had to be kept closed and locked up tightly. Nothing to dare dissention or to threaten the oh-so-perfect heavenly realm. He also discovered her true reason why she had taken up arms and smiled. He'd keep his newfound knowledge tucked tight to himself for now, all the while silently hoping she could give into her true desire.

Armed with the knowledge, he grinned. Careful to remove all traces of his demon-self from her mind, he eased off. All the while, Gareth had been screaming his protest, but Ash got what he needed.

Anya, pale as a snowflake, he eased into a chair. She was unconscious and would wake up deathly sick but with the sisters' healing chants she would heal. Ash didn't feel remorse for his actions. He had gotten what he needed. He picked up the books from the floor and placed them on the table next to her. Anya had a wealth of knowledge held tight in the recesses of her mind and she was an asset he might need again, hence why he took his time to ensure she was okay.

Unlocking the door, Ash quietly exited. He had to get home but knowing Shea was upstairs tucked in bed but wide awake with the feel of night and darkness cascading over her skin made his steps falter. With more willpower than he wanted to exert, Ash forced himself out of the brownstone. No way would he go to his b'iã in Gareth's form. Even though he was demon born, the only arms holding Shea would be his, vowed Ash.

By the blessed light I'm becoming a freaking angel. The cold Boston air surged into his lungs. He was tired. The task of keeping up the façade of being Gareth ate away at him. Ensuring no one was around, he flashed himself home. He surged out of Gareth's body and placed the soldier into a deep sleep. Then he jumped into his fire pit and sighed with pleasure when the hot embers scorched his body. So much of who he was belonged to his father's realm, and even in sleep he sought pain and heat. Telling traits. But power came with pain and his world was heat. To recharge his powers, he had to keep one foot in Lucifer's realm and one on Earth if he was going to invade the Heavens and do the impossible for his b'iã.

CHAPTER ELEVEN

Acclamations of Dissent. Shea wished Ash hadn't shared the knowledge with her. Did she truly want to read all the sins in the Heavens? Shea let her fingertips travel over the spines of the large leather-bound books accumulated in Anya's room. Where did she get them? Shea smiled. Quiet, shy Anya seemed to have developed a book habit. Shea did wonder when Anya had time to search for such treasures and how she knew where to go. At the moment, Anya was sound asleep, oblivious to Shea's presence in her own private room.

At one time Shea might have balked at using her newfound powers to open doors, pick a lock or block a person from seeing her but no more. The shy Shea who would have kept her head down, eyes downcast as befitting an angel sister died the night when her innocence had been taken. In her place, was an angel who strode with purpose, dared anyone to look directly at her and marched into the night like it was her second skin. With the night she felt safe. That too had become something new and she couldn't explain it to any of her angel sisters. She felt their worry like a noose around her neck and it was beginning to suffocate her need for answers. She was changing. Into what? And for what purpose? The Mistress always said all paths had a purpose but how could what had happened to her be a path for good?

When Ash had told her what he'd found out thanks to Anya, Shea had of course needed to push a little more. Anya didn't remember her discourse with Ash. Shea didn't question it but she had certainly asked enough questions to allow Anya to point her in the right direction. Which is why after evening prayers, something she too avoided now, she'd made her way, quiet like a thief in her own house, out the door. She sneaked out of the brownstone and with purpose walked the ten city blocks without a care in the world. It was a revelation to her. The crisp Boston air chilled her but the embrace of the night awoke something dormant within Shea. The place where the book was being kept was in a gray brick building called the Elie Wiesel Center for Judaic Studies, which surprised Shea. How by the blessed light did Anya come to know this? Shea had never seen the young novice leave the house so how did she acquire her knowledge? Electronics, like computers or cellphones, didn't like Shea or any of her fellow fallen angel sisters. In fact, all electrical things seemed to give her shocks so she had made it a habit to avoid them.

Shea used her newfound powers to blend with the shadows and walk without notice through the front door and up the stairs. The place was small but beautiful. The carved woodwork was old and well-polished. A few students were huddled in groups obviously engrossed in their work as no one looked her way when she dared to uncloak herself. Unhindered she made her way upstairs where she sensed the library was housed. On the top floor she found the door; locked. She furrowed her brow deep in thought. She'd never picked a door open and wasn't sure how to proceed when a young man stepped out from a door into the hall, holding a cane.

He turned his head toward her and smiled, and then carefully made his way toward her.

"Sorry, did you want in? I assumed since all the students were downstairs it was time to lock up. Where you searching for something in particular?" he asked, and it was only then Shea realized he was blind but he could sense her, even in her shadow form.

Shea blinked and fought not to turn and run. She'd always avoided humans, and males made her uneasy. Even though he couldn't see her, she had a sense his perception of who she was might be more accurate than the students clustered together downstairs.

"I'm looking for a book," she said.

"This is a great place because we have lots of books. Hope it's old because this library takes antiquity to a whole new meaning," he said, smiling.

He was quite tall and had wheat-colored hair and a dimple revealed its presence on his right cheek. Handsome and wholesome came to mind.

"If you step aside, I will unlock the door for you. You must be new here. I don't recognize you," he said.

"I'm...how could you recognize me. You can't see me," said Shea.

"I might be blind but my other senses are not. You smell like cinnamon and summer and I'm not saying that to embarrass you. I'm Daniel by the way."

"Shea," she answered, smiling. "The cinnamon is because one of my sisters is on a baking rampage and our entire house smells of such."

"You must live in a blessed household for such a feast. I've been here for over a year now and greatly miss my mother's baking."

"You are not from here." She hated how curious she was becoming. She simply needed to get in the library, get the book and end the discussion at once.

"No, I'm from Tel Aviv. My parents sent me here to continue my studies," he said, unlocking the door and easing it open for her to pass by him.

"Studies?"

"I'm attempting to become a Rabbi," he said, giving a slight chuckle.

"There is no greater calling than to teach the Almighty's path of light. Your parents are blessed to have you," said Shea, automatically bowing her head only to realize he couldn't see her action.

"I think you're not from here either. Most of the time when I tell people I feel this calling they laugh at me," he said, stepping into the dark library. He flicked on a light beside the wall for her benefit.

"People will always laugh at things they can't understand. Trust me, I get it. Thank you for unlocking the library."

"Can I help you search for anything?"

"Would it be all right with you if I take my time and have a look around?"

"As you wish. I'll leave you and head back to my office. It's the last door on the right. Just come by when you're done so I can lock up. Nice to meet you, Shea," he said, holding out his hand.

For a second Shea faltered and then her manners kicked in. She took his hand in hers. "The honor is mine. Thank you, Daniel."

He gasped and his grip tightened.

"Is everything all right?" asked Shea, reclaiming her hand.

He nodded his head. "Sorry. Yes, all is good. Don't forget to stop by before you leave."

"Of course," said Shea, watching as he left to shut the door behind him.

Shea took a moment to look around the small library. Most of the books were large volumes and did indeed look ancient. Her fingers trailed over the leathery spines until she found what she was looking for. She eased the book out of the shelf. It was heavy. So heavy it dropped to the floor. For a second Shea worried either Daniel or one of the students would come running to investigate. She held her breath. When no one came she picked up the book and slipped it into her backpack. She waited another ten minutes and then made her way to Daniel's door.

She spotted him at his desk with his earphones in. She knocked on his door. "Thank you."

"Did you find what you were looking for?"

"No but you were very helpful. It was a pleasure to meet you."

"Please don't be a stranger. If I can help in any way please reach out," he said, sliding a business card her way.

"Thank you," she said again accepting the card.

"The pleasure Shea was all mine," said Daniel, standing like a gentleman when she left.

When she walked into the alley, she knew trouble was going to find her but it was the quickest way home.

"Going somewhere, lovely?" asked a man with glowing eyes as he eased out from the back of a dumpster.

A demon. Just what she needed.

Shea stilled, and dared him on. He came closer and then at the last moment she ran like the demons of Hell were on her trail. Quite literally.

He jumped on her back, knocking her to the ground. Her chin took the fall hard and asphalt and skin don't mix. She bled; the sight of her inky black blood shocked her.

The demon laughed. Then in the next instant he was flown across the alley.

"I'd keep your hands to yourself if you want to live," said a woman, shocking Shea. For an instant she thought her savior would be Ash. It was a reminder she needed to learn to fend for herself.

Shea eased up from the dirty asphalt and cupped her bleeding chin.

"Oh, I don't think he's going to like what you did. On second thought, you're dead." The words were no sooner out of the woman's mouth than she used her powers to cause the man to silently scream in agony as flames burst forth from him. Then the woman turned her attention back to Shea.

"So, you are the one he's claimed. Can't say I see the attraction. You're certainly not his type. The little innocent girl act doesn't usually do it for him."

"Excuse me, but who are you?"

"What, no pretty thanks for me saving your skinny ass? Here I thought you angels were all about politeness."

"Guess I've lost my angel edge," said Shea, as she picked up her backpack.

"Ah, I think I'll be taking that," said the woman, who attempted to use her power to wrestle the pack from Shea's hands.

Shea didn't slink out into the night to return empty-handed. With a strength Shea didn't know she possessed she fought for possession of the pack. The woman moved into her space.

"My dear if you think I'm about to let you win this little tug of war, you are sadly mistaken. That is mine."

"No, it's not," said Ash, his voice loud and commanding.

Shea felt a little thrill travel up from her toes to her heart. He materialized at her side, linking his arm with hers. Instant heat eased into her. For a distracted second she wondered if he'd known how cold she'd been. The woman tilted her head and smiled. Goosebumps clamored to life on Shea. She hadn't been afraid of the woman before but she was now. There was something sinister about her smile and in no way did it reach her dark brown eyes.

"Touching, brother dear to see you so enamored of one. What by Satan do you see in this one?"

"Brother?" Shea turned to look at Ash. A mistake. His eyes glowed red. In most cases when he was with her, he'd taken care to hide the demon he truly was but not tonight. Was it wrong Shea found him sinfully beautiful?

"Twice so soon to see you, sister. You must have missed me greatly. Do give my love to father when you see him next, which I am sure will be soon," said Ash.

The woman looked like she'd swallowed nails. Shea didn't dare speak. Something was being said between the two and she knew they were speaking telepathically and her gut said it wasn't civil. In the next instant the woman vanished in a puff of smoke.

Ash turned her into his arms, his heat radiating even more into her chilled bones. "You should not have ventured out on your own."

"That was your sister?"

"Sadly, yes."

"I take it you two don't get along," said Shea, hating that she was burrowing her body into his for more warmth.

He chuckled and tucked her in tight to his body. "That, my b'iã, is an understatement. Why are you out on your own?"

Shea stepped out of his hold. She needed the cold. She had to keep her senses. She had to be the one to take care of herself. Relying on Ash would be her downfall.

"I found the book," she said.

"Why of course you did, my clever girl. I knew you would. Now as much as I like cuddling you in this alley, it's time we go. Let's go back to my place and review it."

His place? Did she want to venture down that road?

"I think I should go home," said Shea.

"Scared my b'iã that I will devour you if you come to my place?"

Shea gulped. She prayed to all the saints he wasn't reading her mind. If he knew what she was thinking she'd burn in Hell. Then again, she'd finally be entering his realm.

"No, that's not it," she said.

Ash grasped her sore chin. "Do not lie to me. You promised me such and I taste the fear in you and while it rubs me the wrong way, I will do the right thing and take you home. This though...this will not do."

And before Shea knew what he was doing the feel of his warm lips slid over hers. She tried not to give in but sacraments were made to be gloriously broken. He pulled her back into his embrace, his arms like molten steel while the taste of his lips like a blessed sacred candle–exotic, refreshing and soothing.

Shea sighed. Ash pulled back. "There my b'iã, much better. You were made in the image of perfection and the sight of you scarred is not to my liking."

Automatic, her hand went to her chin. Of course, he'd healed her. She should hate him for his act of kindness but it was those very acts making her question the demon who had stolen her innocence and vowed to make the world right for her. She should hate him. She should loathe him and want nothing to do with him but those small acts, so out of character, unsettled her enough to believe in the Mistress' message. If she could get him to save her sister was it wrong to want to hope the demon he was could change?

She slid the backpack onto her shoulder. "You didn't need to heal me."

"Need and want, my b'iã, are two very different things," said Ash, linking his arm through hers as they sauntered from the alley back to her brownstone.

CHAPTER TWELVE

Izzy ached. Who knew she'd have a sparring session with the Doyen. Better yet who knew the Doyen could discard her Chanel business suits for jiu-jitsu gear or that she'd have a deadly aim. Izzy eased her arms into a sweater as she composed her thoughts. Lilith. The name evoked memories of time in school learning lessons about the sins of mankind. The recurring theme–the evolution of sin was because of Lilith. She rubbed her temples and was sorely tempted to seek the hands of Nathanael who knew exactly which pressure points to press on her body to ease comfort. He too was an enigma. A warrior who she was bound to, he was waiting...letting her make the move and set the pace in their relationship. It went against everything he'd been taught but it certainly was winning her over. Not as if she'd let on.

A gentle knock on the door let her know Meredith was on the other side.

"Come in," she answered, smiling when the heated scent of hot chocolate filled her room.

"I thought you could use this," said Meredith, placing the steaming mug on the table next to Izzy as she claimed the chair.

"Thank you," said Izzy.

Meredith had her own sweet delight–a cup of white-hot chocolate. They sat in silence, each savoring the hot liquid but Izzy knew she had to share her knowledge.

"Meredith, do you remember your teachings of Lilith?"

Meredith's eyebrows drew sharply together. "Of course. Why?"

"What if we weren't told the entire truth?" said Izzy, taking a sip of the hot chocolate.

Meredith moved to perch on the edge of the chair, her drink discarded. "What did you learn, Isabella?"

Izzy leaned forward. "I met with the Doyen of the house. The Earth-angels are all sisters of Lilith–she is their creator. Each of them came to the point of death and she offered them a choice. I should say they also committed heinous crimes but still she gave them a choice...life in servitude to her or death."

"I cannot fathom Sky or Winter committing a crime, let alone one to be defined as heinous," said Meredith, clearly echoing Izzy's earlier thoughts.

"I agree. Seems impossible but sadly it would appear so. Most choose life. She taught the Doyen to fight and they have a stockpile of weapons I admit to being envious of."

"Weapons? Where? As I recall I only saw rooms where they pampered themselves."

Izzy smiled, indicating to Meredith to take a sip of her drink. "They, like us, are masters of illusion. Trust me, the Doyen might rock any board room but she's no princess in the ring. That woman can fight. She's well over two hundred years old."

"You are kidding me!"

"No. I did sense there were things she was not speaking to keep the truth from me but what truly matters is they have weapons and know how to fight."

"Then why are they acting like they can't?"

Ah, the crux of things. "The Doyen gave them instructions to play like they don't know how to fight until she knew the stakes."

"I bet the same can be said of the boys."

"I would assume but alas when I pressed her about the Earth-bound angels who are males she wouldn't speak. I was assured they were not created by Lilith."

Meredith leaned back fully in her chair, cupping her mug. "This is all very confusing. Why would Lilith create female Earth-angels, and who is responsible for creating the males? I think we should find out."

"Honestly all I want is for them to fight like they know how. I need to see progress. The Doyen has assured me they will all attend the next training session. I told her about Lucifer's army amassing and she wasn't surprised."

"Do you think Lilith acts like our Mistress for them?"

"Yes. When I asked the Doyen if she'd like to speak with our Mistress she practically fell to her knees in supplication."

"Interesting. Guess Lilith didn't relate how much the Mistress and her do not get along."

"Considering there has been a chasm of over a thousand heavenly years between them that is an understatement."

"And what of Winter? Can she be saved?"

"To heal an earth-born angel poisoned with hellfire we need demon blood. We need their help. They are loyal to Lilith and I am worried our Mistress would not be pleased with our act," said Izzy.

"We must do whatever we can to save her, Izzy."

Izzy nodded. "I am in agreement."

"Surely our Mistress knows how earth-born angels are made," said Meredith.

"I think not. I think this has been a closely-guarded secret."

Meredith took a long sip of her drink and then got up to pace the small room. "But Lilith and the Mistress, if I recall correctly, are true blood sisters."

"As you well know not all sisters have a faithful or good relationship. It doesn't matter, the Doyen has agreed to help us to save Winter. But..." paused Izzy.

"But what?"

"Only if we promise not to speak of this to the Mistress. They took an oath to Lilith and I will not push this. I have offered to broker a meeting between our Doyen and the Mistress but I will leave it up to the Doyen to speak on this matter."

"You think such a move wise?"

"It's the only way," said Izzy.

Meredith sighed. "I am not sure this secret can be kept. The Mistress can easily read us all."

"We must try. The Doyen is coming tonight with the tools we require to capture a demon. We have only this night. By tomorrow morning it will be too late for Winter."

Meredith nodded. "I will inform the others and you must tell the earth-born angels we know they can fight true. To think all this time, they have been faking it makes me sick."

"It made my day. You do recall how Gareth pushed them over and over again. Now it makes me smile."

Meredith chuckled. "Well, when you put it that way, I do see your point. Tonight, though, is serious business."

"It is, Meredith. We must capture a demon to save her and this shall not be an easy task."

"Since coming to Earth over a decade ago, nothing has been easy so why would this be any different?" said Meredith.

Izzy said nothing. They both finished their hot drink, relishing the silence, knowing tonight the game had to change in their favor or they would lose a sister to a fate worse than death.

CHAPTER THIRTEEN

The Doyen entered through the front door dressed to kill. Manicured fingers, hair neatly tied back all the while wearing a white Chanel suit with four-inch matching heels. Shea watched from the sidelines. She'd been forced to attend the meeting with all her sisters but she had chosen to enter at the last moment, leaving her the closest to the exit. Upstairs, tucked into her room, Ash was reviewing the book. He'd tried to take it with him back to his place but they had quickly discovered he couldn't touch the pages without them catching fire. Even wearing gloves hadn't done the trick. Shea had thought Ash would be infuriated, but he'd laughed it off and kissed her knuckles saying it allowed him access to her because she had to dutifully turn the pages for him. Astonished, Shea had smiled. A demon teasing, again not something she could easily wrap her mind around.

The Doyen stood in the middle of the room. All the Earth-bound angels stood at the ready for their Doyen, making it clear to Shea where their true loyalty lay.

"I have examined Winter and she doesn't have much time. Tonight, to save her she needs demon blood," said the Doyen.

Not a sound could be heard. They'd all been trained to keep surprise tightly leashed.

"She will need to have her blood removed and a transfusion of demon blood and then she will need to drink holy water. It will not be easy for her. Alas, it is the only way to save her soul," said the Doyen, taking time to slowly let her haughty gaze linger on all of them.

"I have spoken with Isabella and she knows your true skills, daughters," said the Doyen.

Daughters? Shea found the word intriguing but again wore her impartial face. She did not want to draw attention to herself and clung to the shadow cresting the room, letting them all know dusk was settling.

Isabella moved from her spot to stand next to the Doyen. A smile lit her face. "Imagine my delight to learn you all have skills and better yet weapons, which will make a difference in this war. No longer will we take it easy on you. Tonight, by the blessing of your Doyen you are tasked to capture a demon–not score a kill."

"The Doyen has brought five blessed nets which will aid us. I will claim one, Meredith the other, Zachary and Gareth will have one and Sky will have the last. Our goal is to save Winter tonight. I have faith we will accomplish our task but this will not be easy. Demon blood is poisonous. Do not let a drop mar thy flesh. I have one net left and ask for a volunteer in this blessed quest," said Isabella.

Shea stepped from the shadow. "I will claim the net."

The Doyen turned her head to examine Shea but it was Isabella who moved toward her.

"Shea, I am delighted you are feeling more like yourself but this task might be too much."

Shea was not like her old self; a truism she could not voice. "Let me help. I need..."

The Doyen stepped forward. "Your sister has spoken and there is strength in stepping forward and honor in wanting to help. She will be most welcomed."

For a moment Shea thought Isabella might voice displeasure. She stepped closer to Shea and for a heartbeat fear skirted through Shea. Would Isabella touch her? Isabella leaned closer. "Are thee sure?"

Shea nodded.

Isabella stood straighter. "We are honored Shea, our sister, will join us tonight in our quest to save Winter. Now it is time for us to seek the demon. Thank you, Doyen for your help in this matter."

The Doyen nodded and Isabella ushered her out of the room. Everyone immediately filed out like toy soldiers eager for their task.

Shea stepped into the hall, prepared to go back to her room and change into more appropriate attire for battle.

"Shea, thank you for stepping forward to help," said the Doyen, her voice surprising Shea, who had assumed she'd vacated the brownstone.

"It is my honor to lend aid," said Shea.

The Doyen stepped closer to Shea and it took iron will not to race upstairs to the safety of Ash.

"Your hair is an unusual color for an angel."

Shea clenched her teeth and felt her heart flutter. What to say? It was Meredith who came to her rescue.

"Sorry to interrupt, Doyen, but Shea must change before prayer and Isabella would like to introduce you to Zachary," stated Meredith.

The Doyen tilted her head and nodded. "Again, Shea thank you for stepping into the light to help."

Shea nodded and then quickly made her way upstairs. At the top of the stairs, she wasn't surprised to discover Ash in his shadow form. She'd sensed him the moment he had vacated her room.

"She has upset you," stated Ash.

Shea surprised herself. She reached out and touched his face. He leaned into her hand. Heat swept through her.

"I am fighting tonight."

Ash captured her hand in his and said nothing as he moved her back into the privacy of her room.

Only once she was safely in the room did he turn his full attention to her.

"Why must you feel the need to fight?"

That was the question roaring through Shea every second of the day now.

"I need to feel useful." The moment Shea spoke the words she knew to her core, a pull for more out of life was the essence of her restlessness.

Ash pulled her to him. "You are more useful than you will ever know. I found something in the book, my b'iã. I believe I know where your sister is and better yet, I know a way into the realm to save her."

Shea let Ash hug her as tears silently flowed. She'd question her actions later. He cupped her chin and forced her to look at him.

"It will not be easy," he said.

"Do what you must," said Shea.

"And you my b'iã will not let a scratch mar thy skin tonight. Demon hunting is not meant for you and I can attest to it."

He was teasing her again. It truly was a miraculous night.

"Shea take this," said Ash, handing her a small knife with a solid ruby ornamentally decorating the hilt. "This is a special knife and will aid you in your quest. But, I confess, I will not be a happy demon if you are harmed. I must go tonight to make my attempt as the window of opportunity is slim."

Shea smiled up at him. "Thank you for your attempt and your belief in me."

"Never doubt yourself, Shea. You are a powerful angel and what has been done to you and your sister is not right."

Shea felt the tears threaten again but held them in check. A demon spoke the truth of what had become her life and this demon who had claimed her vowed to make amends. Shea's teachings told her not to trust a demon but then again, her teachings told her, her twin didn't exist. That lie felt like dirt in her mouth, bitter and foul.

A knock at her door interrupted her thoughts.

"Shea, are you ready?" asked one of her sisters.

"Give me a moment," said Shea, moving out of Ash's embrace.

"You need to leave. I need to change," said Shea.

He smiled; his eyes turned red; it should have scared her. It didn't. "I will leave you to get ready, my b'iã and promise to only return to you when I have your sister safely in my hands."

Ash bowed low, honoring his pledge and then in a puff, disappeared.

Shea smiled and then quickly changed. She tucked his gift into the waist of her pants needing to feel the heat of the knife against her skin. She tied her long hair into a tight ponytail and savored the feel of the night.

Opening her door, she joined her sisters in the prayer room and for once felt at peace. How ironic it took marching into a fight to find such relief.

CHAPTER FOURTEEN

The crisp of the night made her skin tight and Meredith was on edge. Her mood was not improved with Zachary at her side. She didn't want him anywhere within her vision. She had two Earth-angels to contend with and a demon they had to capture. Zachary's presence was a huge distraction Meredith tried to ignore, and failed. She never thought to see Zachary clothed in jeans and a black biker jacket. The teens today would say he was lit or hot and both adjectives aptly described him.

"Meredith you take the alley to the right," commanded Zachary.

The alley, brightly lit with a neon bowling sign, would be useless. The chances of securing a demon there screamed zero.

Meredith had memorized the area they were tasked with patrolling. "No. We will take the alley to the left at the next block. That alley is too bright and no demons will come."

Zachary froze. He turned to look at her and Meredith fought not to lower her eyes or bow her head.

"I think we should break into two teams for a better chance to secure the demon," stated Zachary.

Meredith stopped walking. *He wants to separate us because he doesn't think we should be hunting a demon.* The knowledge burned deep within Meredith.

"Zachary, that is not the plan set in motion. We agreed to go as one team to use each net to secure a demon. It's the strategy we discussed with Isabella."

"Plans change," he said gruffly.

"Yes, that can be the case but for now it is not needed. We will stick to the original plan."

"Meredith are you arguing with me?" asked Zachary, casting her a look she couldn't decipher.

"Arguing?" *Wouldn't dare.* "Hardly. Stating a fact. The plan is a good one. We move forward with it," stated Meredith, feeling annoyed.

Zachary moved closer to her. "As you demand," he said, mockingly but there was a smile to his lips she'd never seen before.

Before she resumed her march into the dark alley, Zachary stepped into her personal space. "Earth has changed you, Meredith."

"Yes, Zachary, it has," said Meredith, stepping around to be the leader to charge into the dark alley to secure the demon.

For a moment, Meredith could have sworn she heard Zachary say, "I like it," but such was probably a wishful prayer.

Meredith was in the middle and the two young angels flanked either side. Zachary was in the back, and she highly suspected he was fuming with his new position. They slinked into the inky black of the night and only when they were out of sight did Meredith draw the knife she'd sequestered.

"What are you doing?" asked one of the earth-born angels.

"Getting what we came here for tonight," said Meredith.

The second earth-born angel, the one who Meredith knew could aim throwing stars with dead accuracy, reached into her backpack to withdraw the net. "I agree. Why search for demons when we can make them come to us?"

Meredith smiled. She was starting to like these earth-born angels.

"Do not," whispered Zachary.

Meredith was tired of his assuming authority over her. She turned, ensuring he could view her action and with a nod of her head, slashed her hand, letting the golden-hued blood drop to the pavement. Within five seconds the scent of sulfur filled the alley.

"That wasn't smart," said Zachary.

"Smarts have nothing to do with catching demons," said the earth-born angel with the net. She grinned when they all sensed the demons coming.

Meredith smiled. "Guess we got their attention."

A second later the three of them were fighting off six demons. Twice Meredith had to fend off two demons at once and her sword arm she was wielding was starting to ache. "Throw the net," shouted Meredith.

The twirling sound alerted Meredith that her instructions were being followed.

The screaming howl as the net captured a demon filled the alley like an operatic song. Within minutes the other teams arrived on the scene.

Ensuring the demon was fully wrapped in the net as a captured fish, Isabella stuffed a rag into the howling demon's mouth to shut her up and threw a blanket over her. They strode from the alley like they were play acting a theater performance with their prize, the rolled-up blanket, to ensure their street drama wasn't seen as anything out of the ordinary. Once at the brownstone, they all hustled inside. Isabella removed the blanket and then they dropped the still-thrashing demon next to the bed by Winter.

Isabella secured the demon with gold cuffs to ensure she couldn't escape.

Shea knew the demon's scent. She moved closer into the room. She looked down at the demon and realized it was

Ash's sister. Glad a rag kept the demon from saying anything, Shea slunk out of the room. She needed space to think. They were planning to give Winter, Ash's sister, demon blood and then kill her. Could Shea let that happen to his sister when Ash was planning a way to save her twin? Not knowing what to do, Shea scurried back to her room. She needed to pray and for once was fearful she'd lost the knack.

CHAPTER FIFTEEN

T he air was brittle and cold. Not a place for a demon of Hell. Ash materialized inside the place eerily known as The Precipice. The ground was of ice, and there were two black mountains with what looked like carved steel doors cut into the folds of their crevices. Each door was about thirty feet in height yet strangely narrow, only about four feet wide, which would allow only one or two people at a time to enter. The landscape was sparse and only a few jagged rocks providing insufficient cover allowed Ash to get his bearings. The moment Ash had materialized, he'd felt drained. The power of Heaven fueled this gray eerie place and the longer Ash stayed the more his demon powers would weaken. He had to find a way inside and after roughly guessing each mountain had over a hundred doors, he had to find the one housing Shea's sister. There was no doubt in his mind, behind each door was a prison cell. He'd been in too many not to mistake a solid door for its true purpose–keeping those inside from escaping.

His heightened hearing heard the squeak of hinges in need of oil and then his eyes noticed a door, about half-way up the second mountain, moving. Going on instinct, he ran across the frozen ground and then using the momentum of his wings he jumped up to where the door was opening, catching the startled angel completely off-guard.

"What?" said the female angel, attempting to speak.

"I am looking for a twin?" said Ash, pushing his blade against the angel's pale neck.

The angel attempted to speak and Ash realized he'd have to relax his hold and the knife to understand her words.

"Which one?"

It took Ash's brain about thirty seconds to fully understand the angel's words. Which one? Behind each door was a twin? Behind each door was evidence of the 'stain'. Behind each door was concrete proof of heavenly lies.

Knowing he couldn't save them all, especially since he felt his powers draining at an accelerating rate, he turned the angel around and looked her in the eye. "The one born of Shea."

She blinked but then notched up her chin. "You are too late."

He'd be the judge. "Tell me which door is her prison or I will kill you."

"She is over there, the fourth row, thirteenth door. As I said, you are too late. She succumbed as was her rightful duty."

For a moment, Ash thought the angel would say, "about time," because those were the words of omission he heard in her voice. The knowledge she'd been kept in a cell all her life did something to Ash he wasn't proud of. Without taking his eyes from the angel, he slid the blade across her neck. She blinked at him in surprise and then pitched backward, landing with a thud on the frozen turf.

Ash flew to his destination and yanked open the door of the cell. There curled up in a corner with a cerecloth as her only cover was Shea's sister. He yanked off the cloth, hating the feel of the wax on his palm. The site of the female angel who had been deprived of so much shocked him. She was skeleton-thin and wrapped like the dead. They had even shaved her hair off. Ash felt a grief so profound he yearned to burn the mountains down. Returning with Shea's dead twin, which he'd known was a possibility, angered him. With a trembling hand, he reached out and picked her up to cradle her to his chest. Her limbs hung like dangling twigs and her head loosely fell back on him. She weighed next to nothing. In picking her up, he realized something. She wasn't quite dead. A pulse, so faint, one could barely discern, he heard with his demon senses and more importantly he knew her soul while starting the journey to the afterlife, could still be pulled back. With a new sense of hope, he shook off his jacket and draped it over her naked form. With one last look at her cell, he noticed the etchings on the wall. She must have used a rock to carve the drawings and if Shea could see them, her heart would weep. Shea's twin had used what little energy she'd had to create her own garden of Eden. Every wall was etched with flowers and trees. It was a beautiful sad scene in what had to be her life lived in a Hell, sadly putting the word Heaven to shame. In that moment, Ash realized something. His own father's twin had been housed in a cell like this before he'd been broken free by Lucifer and an odd sense of respect for his demon father welled up in his chest.

"Don't you dare die on me now for my Shea would hate me for eternity," said Ash, as he prepared to jump from the mountain with his slight burden. "I know you are tough, just like your twin, so I beg of you. Fight for your life. We're leaving this place for good and I want you to meet your twin, Shea."

Ash had hoped his speech might inspire a response. Getting none, he jumped from the mountain, skidding to a stop on the frozen ground but not before he'd torn the skin from his right knee. He wondered why no alarm sounded. In the next instant he knew why. A dozen armed angels flew at him. Holding his bundle closer, he darted and dove as they threw spears at him. He was tiring but he had less than five hundred feet until he made it back to the portal. Going on his reserves, he saw the portal up ahead. Ash took a giant leap, needing the momentum as he flung his wings out to push through the portal. He felt a piercing pain slam into him but in the next instant the heat of his home engulfed him.

"Well, if it isn't my dear lost son," said Lucifer, who was the last demon Ash had hoped to see.

Ash tried to speak but before he could, his father leaned closer.

"Save your energy. You are going to need it. My, what is this delight?" asked Lucifer reaching out to take Shea's twin sister from his grip.

Ash tried to stop his father. Lucifer snapped his fingers.

"Fix my son. He and I have a lot to catch up on," said Lucifer, walking away with his prized possession.

The last thought before Ash finally succumbed to the blackness as pain washed over him in radiating coldness was, he could have sworn he'd seen his father look with a softness, almost a pitying expression, but it couldn't be. His father, the king of Hell, did not pity anyone, least of all a soon-to-be dead angel.

When next Ash awoke, he was surprised to discover he was in his boyhood bed. A servant handed him a flaming drink, which he didn't hesitate to down. Immediate heat filled him, making him feel marginally better.

Only when the servant left, did Ash realize he wasn't alone.

"Father?" he called out to the room, as the smoke coalesced into Lucifer.

His father came to his side. Ash tried to get out of bed, but realized then something wet and sticky had been placed on his back.

"You almost died," stated Lucifer.

It was on the tip of Ash's tongue to ask, "What would it matter?" Wisely, he kept the wisecrack to himself. He managed to sit. "Where is she?"

Lucifer quirked an eyebrow at him. "Why, son, are you always testing me?"

Ash laughed. He couldn't help himself. His entire life had been nothing but a test, one set by his own demon father.

"I guess I'm a sucker for punishment. Where is she and how long have I been out?

"She is healing. You've been testing my patience for almost two days."

Two days? Ash tried not to panic. He wondered what had happened with Gareth. His control over his body and mind couldn't hold for that amount of time. He longed to see Shea's twin but didn't dare voice his desire. He pulled the wet thing off his back, praying it had healed his wings and swung his legs over the side of the bed. "What have you done with her?"

Lucifer held out his hands. "Nothing. You brought an almost dead angel into my realm, which I don't know to be pleased about or angry, but you can rest assured the young lady I would not harm. She has already met with enough harm for an eternity."

With shaky legs, Ash got to his feet. "You know."

"Know what?"

"I found her at the place your twin was held."

Lucifer paced the floor. "What you say is impossible."

Ash quickly told his father about The Precipice and the hundreds of prison cells. "I never believed your story but now I know the validity of your truth."

"Son, I never told you my story."

"No, but others made sure I knew. Did you think as your son I wouldn't want to know of your origin? I too, had a thirst for knowledge and it's led me to this discovery."

"Is that all it has led you to, son?" asked Lucifer, quietly.

Omission worked the same way for demons as angels. "I heard about the place and had to see for my own eyes."

"Ah," said Lucifer. "And you simply had to rescue one?"

"They thought her dead. I knew better. I thought she wouldn't be missed."

Lucifer turned to the fire and held out his hands to the flames, which arched like pets seeking a caress. "Yes, she was and they came after you. Why risk your life for hers?"

Ash couldn't formulate a response but luckily, he was saved from answering when a demon rushed into the room.

The demon crouched at Lucifer's feet. "Your daughter is missing."

Lucifer snarled. The demon cowered and Ash knew enough to keep his distance. The king of Hell had a nasty temper and didn't like surprises.

"What say you? Explain."

"Kali insisted on leading the demons to Earth and only two returned. One said she was captured by a net."

It was never a good sign when his father turned to smoke. The demon tried to crawl out the door but a smoke-formed hand choked the life out of him before he could flee.

"Let me help find her, father," said Ash, wondering if he truly had a death wish.

His father's smoky form coalesced into his solid one, so Ash pressed on. "I have a feeling I might know where she is. Let me bring her back to Hell."

"What is it with you children these days?" said Lucifer. "Fine. Return her to me or else."

In the next instant Ash was alone in his room. The 'or else' didn't need to be explained. His father had a creative mind when it came to torture. Moving on unsteady legs, Ash turned his body to smoke and willed himself to his own residence. Gareth was nowhere to be seen, which didn't surprise Ash. Using his senses, he tried to pinpoint him but he got nothing. He couldn't walk into Shea's residence as it was safeguarded with protection wards and more importantly Isabella would enjoy removing his head with one of her special swords. What he could do was reach out to Shea in the hopes she might help. After all, he'd risked everything for her twin. He almost laughed. She'd say he'd created his own Hell and she'd be correct.

CHAPTER SIXTEEN

Meredith didn't want to kill the demon. Killing was a sin. She didn't dare voice her objection to Isabella who was solely focused on the mission–save Winter, at all costs.

"You have caught a demon of high-ranking," said the Doyen.

Her unusual statement quelled the whispering in the room. Meredith walked over to the Doyen. "How do you know?"

"She has the highborn etchings marked into her skin. She's worked her way up the demon ranks."

Isabella moved to Meredith's other side. "Demon ranks?" stated Isabella, looking for the first time at the scars etched all over the demon's skin.

"This." The Doyen pointed to a star dug deep into the right side of her forehead. "Is unusual. I can't recall a demon with a star etching, but I will consult the books. As for these," the Doyen pointed out three other etching, one a triangle sitting upside down on her throat, the other a set of small circles with lines drawn through them located on the demon's right shoulder and a dozen small lines formed almost a linked belt below her bellybutton.

"These are small kills," said the Doyen, pointing out the belt of lines. "This means she's killed at least three angel warriors," she said, holding her finger above the cluster of circles and when she almost touched the upside down triangle, she said. "This means she's killed a jinn, one who could evoke incantations and move between Earth and Hell. Trust me, you have captured a highly prized demon."

"Should we be worried?" asked Meredith. Knowing now the type of demon they'd captured and brought to their residence, did not rest easy with Meredith.

"No demon can enter our house, Meredith. Plus, we don't have time to worry. Anya, you need to set up the transfusion. We need to get this started."

Meredith and the Doyen backed away to allow Anya and Sky to set up the equipment for the blood transfusion.

Meredith edged closer to the back of the room. "By putting the blood from Winter into the demon, we're killing the demon, right?"

The Doyen turned and looked at her. "I don't know. When this was done for me, I was unconscious. I don't truly know what happened to the demon."

"You are saying, there is a chance we won't have to kill the demon?"

Both Isabella and the Doyen gave her a piercing look. "No," they said in unison.

"Meredith, the demon must be killed," answered Zachary. "We can't risk the demon returning to Hell to detail any information about your safehouse."

Well, when he put it like that, it did make sense.

Nathanael edged closer to Isabella. "Meredith, we've been killing demons for nights now. This is no different."

Killing demons who were trying to kill you felt different, thought Meredith. She nodded, keeping her disquiet to herself.

"We're ready," said Sky and with a click of a switch blood went from the demon into Winter and vice versa.

"I think I will go to the prayer room," said Meredith, feeling oddly disturbed by the proceedings.

"Good idea," said Isabella, leading the way.

"You will call us if you need anything," said Isabella to Anya.

So much for some alone time. Meredith trailed after the small crowd, leaving Anya to her task. Only when they were kneeling in prayer did Meredith realize Shea was no longer with them. At least one of us managed to escape for some solitude.

Bowing her head in much-needed prayer, Meredith tried to focus on the purity of her thoughts. The task was impossible. Kneeling next to her was Zachary himself. After an hour of what felt like a futile mission, Meredith excused herself.

"Meredith, a word," said Zachary the moment she got into the hall.

Not wanting to turn around to his typical command, Meredith did as instructed. She was tired after a busy day and night and not up to a verbal sparring match with Zachary.

"Yes," said Meredith, keeping her distance. If he wanted to talk, he'd be the one walking her way. Hoping he'd simply say goodnight, she was surprised when he sauntered toward her.

"Would you spare me a few minutes of your time?"

She almost laughed. Time, on Earth, they had aplenty. "But of course."

"Let's go to the kitchen. I shall endeavor to make us something hot to drink."

The almighty Zachary in the kitchen? This Meredith had to see. It was times like this she wished with all her might she could use a cell phone to record what surely had to be a historic moment in time. To have something she could watch over and over again detailing Zachary doing a task normally expected of a Cherub would be her prized possession.

She smiled and let him lead the way, thinking that this day had to be the most significant date ever.

CHAPTER SEVENTEEN

Lucifer eyed the child-woman, understanding her pain. It was a constant ache he'd consumed since his origins. He'd thought his burning down the place where his twin had been exiled to had put an end to Heaven's subterfuge, as he'd been foretold, but it too was a bitter lie. The truth lay shivering before him.

"I will not harm you," said Lucifer.

The child-woman said nothing as her body tried to find comfort. Her soul, barely tethered to her, was waning. The female would die. That statement was probably already Scripture in some heavenly tomb and the injustice of it slammed into the God of Hell.

The crimes he'd supposedly committed in his former life, had made him what he had become–a God; all because he dared to love his twin and try to save him. Lucifer took another perusal of the female shivering uncontrollably on the bed. Dare he give her the choice? He wasn't a God to ponder things, more a being of action, consequences-bedamned, but for the tiny female who had endured so much in such a short time he felt the need to offer a choice.

He leaned closer to her. "I can offer you life, but you will be tied to me for eternity."

No response. He waited another minute and was about to turn from the bed when he heard the soft whisper.

"Yes," she said.

The mere task of answering his question had cost her what little energy she had, but Lucifer had heard. He grinned. The female had courage and for her fortification he'd do right by her.

"This my dear will hurt."

For a second he could have sworn she'd said, "What's new?"

Trying to be gentle, when everything in his being was meant for much more, was tasking for Lucifer. Still though he gathered her shivering form to his, letting his heat finally engulf her.

"Ahh," she said, sighing in content.

Lucifer was about to sink his fangs into her neck to tie her to him but at the last moment he surprised himself. He tilted her head and kissed her, breathing a part of his essence into her, gifting her immortality and so much more than she could have dared to dream.

When the connection was finally sealed, he released her, easing her down to the bed. A blinding flash of heat was the only warning as her body erupted in flames while she screamed to the Heavens for death.

The change wasn't long, but Lucifer knew if felt like eternity for her. He took a step closer to the bed once things settled. The child-woman was gone and in her place was a woman equal to him. Her skin was the color of ivory and she was six feet in height, with hair turned white with a black streak down the middle he found oddly endearing. Her figure was full and lush.

She opened her eyes. They were the blue of robin eggs, a heavenly gift, which he liked.

"Thank you," she said.

Lucifer tucked the blanket around her. "My pleasure. Can you tell me your name?"

She pulled the blanket to her chin. "I am no one."

He did not like her statement. He too, recalled another saying those same hurtful words.

"Trust me you are not no one," said Lucifer. With a wave of his hands, he clothed her. She gasped and then he watched her dainty hands trail over the fabric.

"Are you the God of Hell?"

"Yes."

She eased from the blanket to sit and then mustered her strength to stand.

"Why did you save me?"

"Because I understand your pain."

Her blue eyes assessed him. She took two steps toward him and then surprised him by reaching up to touch his face. He hadn't bothered to mask himself. He rarely did when in his own domain but he wondered what she thought.

"Yes, I see the truth of your words. I had no idea you would be so beautiful," she said, cupping his face in her hands.

"You knew of me?"

"Only whispers of your existence. I am forever grateful you saved me but I'm not sure why."

Truthfully, neither was he. "My son brought you here."

She took another tiny step toward him. "I must say my thanks to him. But first I want to know all about you."

About him? Lucifer took a step back but then braced himself. He was the God of Hell but there was something in her tenderness of him which unsettled him.

Lucifer found himself sitting on the bed and telling her things he'd told no one. She didn't say much. When had her hand found his, he thought, liking the contrast of her pale skin next to his much darker shade.

"I am the God of Hell for a reason," said Lucifer.

"It sounds to me like you weren't given the choice. Much like my existence. I too was left to die because of my twin."

"I killed my twin."

"I am not one to judge. You have given me life when others tried to end it. For such you have my loyalty."

"It was my pleasure. Now do you feel up to a tour of my domain?"

She smiled and Lucifer could have sworn a slice of Heaven shone on her. Not releasing her hand, he eased her more to his side. She linked her arm in his.

"Why do I feel such a connection to you?"

Lucifer wanted to lie to her but they'd kept to the truth so far. "To keep you alive I gave a part of myself to you."

She tilted her head to the side. "Am I to understand you sacrificed a part of yourself for my life?"

Her statement made him sound heroic. "Yes."

She turned to him and then reached up to let her fingers trace his lips. Lucifer felt the horns on his head heat up. No one looked at the true face of the devil with fondness but she did.

"I want a name. Will you help me?"

Giving her hand a squeeze, he replied. "Most certainly. Now, if you have the strength, let me show you around. You must be famished."

She laughed. The sound went straight to Lucifer's heart, which he'd thought long dead.

"Did you make a joke?"

It took him a second to see her reasoning and once he did, he too laughed. All the years his twin had been caged he too had been starved, as had she. "I guess I did." Lucifer moved her closer to him. "Trust me, you will never feel hunger again."

"Or the cold," she said, smiling. "For that alone, I want to kiss you."

"Kiss me?"

She turned into his embrace and once again cupped his face. "Yes, kiss you."

Temptation was something the God of Hell loved.

CHAPTER EIGHTEEN

S hea didn't know what to do. Yes, they needed to save Winter but not by killing Ash's sister. This she could not allow. However, she didn't know how to stop things. She twisted a piece of her hair in angst.

"Shea, thank you so much for your courage tonight," said Isabella, striding out of the room which housed Winter and the demon. For the barest of glimpses, Shea saw the two lying on beds side by side.

"My pleasure to help. How is Winter?"

Isabella smiled. "I have faith she is on the mend. She seems to be handling the transfusion and the Doyen said the worst was almost over. Now it is up to her."

"And the demon?"

"Hopefully dead soon. I wish I felt a bit of remorse with those words but I would be lying. The more dead demons, the better for us."

"Yes of course," said Shea.

"Did you see where Meredith went?"

"I believe she is in the kitchen with Zachary. I overhead him offering to make her a hot beverage."

"He offered to make her a drink? His limited time on Earth seems to be changing him rapidly. I'm not sure I view this as a good thing."

Shea moved closer to the room where Winter was battling for her life. "Time on this Earth has changed us all."

Isabella gave her a look; one Shea didn't want to examine too closely. "Would you mind if I went in to say a prayer for Winter?"

"Shea, your offer would be a true blessing. I'm off to talk with Meredith. Do let me know if there is any change."

Shea nodded and then watched Isabella march toward the kitchen. Marching was Isabella's version of walking. She was always a full stride ahead. It was a quality which had endeared Shea to her all those years ago when she'd sought out females to the cause for justice. Slipping quietly into the room, it took Shea a moment to realize she wasn't alone. The Doyen sat perched on a chair in the corner.

"It's Shea, correct?"

"Yes, Doyen. I heard from Isabella things are going well for Winter."

The Doyen got up and came to where Shea stood next to Winter's bed. "I am beyond pleased."

"And the demon?"

"Do not be afraid. She can't hurt you or anyone else. It is a matter of minutes before death consumes her."

"What happens when she dies?"

"She will turn to ashes. It's the way of demons."

The Doyen was about to say more when her cell chimed. "Excuse me. I must take this. You don't mind me leaving you here, alone do you?"

"No, I am fine. You will have better reception in the hall."

The Doyen nodded with understanding as she quickly exited the room. The curse of being an angel meant electrical devices like cellphones or computers went haywire. Their brownstone was equipped with electricity but it was a constant battle to replace bulbs. Most of the angels had lamps in their rooms and the kitchen had a natural gas oven. Shea speculated their bodies gave off electrical energy which reacted with Earth's energy.

Shea looked at Ash's sister. Her skin, once cinnamon-colored, looked the dull casting of ash.

Lost in her thoughts, it took Shea a few seconds to realize Ash was throwing rocks at the bedroom window. She quickly opened the window. "Stop. What are you doing?"

"Invite me in, Shea?"

Instinctively, Shea moved from the window. He was in solid form. She knew what he was asking. Her invite would grant him access.

"I beg of you," said Ash into her mind.

Shea knew time was of the essence. Moving back to the window she called out, "Ash, please come to me."

A blink and he was by her side. She expected him to immediately rally around his sister. Surprising her his arms engulfed her in a much-needed warming hug. "Oh, how I have missed you. I don't have much time, but I have good news for you. I found your sister. She is safe. I will tell you all later but I must remove Kali. Seems to me lately, I'm saving sisters."

Shea felt numb. "You found my sister?"

"Yes. I will explain all later. You must unhook her from the angel. If I touch the thing," said Ash pointing to the plastic tubing connecting the two bodies. "I'm likely to make it melt."

Shea did as instructed, removing first the needle from Winter and then Kali. She had a dozen questions zinging through her head but she also knew they had limited time alone. The Doyen was still on her cell, but Shea feared the conversation wouldn't last long.

Ash scooped up his sister. "How will you explain she's missing?"

He is always thinking of my welfare. Shea smiled. "Leave such to me. Come back tonight and tell me all about my sister. You must go."

"Not without a kiss."

"A kiss? You're kidding."

"No, I fear I am not. You provide me with strength and I yearn for the taste of you."

He should have been a poet. Shea moved closer to him and then gave him a quick peck on the cheek.

"That doesn't count," said Ash.

"You didn't specify what type of kiss or where. I did as you asked. Now go."

Ash grinned. "Next time I will be quite specific. Please be safe."

"I will," said Shea.

In a blink they were both gone. Shea didn't know what to do. How would she explain the vanished demon? She looked around the room and it was then she noticed the fireplace. Moving fast, she grasped a couple handfuls of ash from the cold fire and tossed them onto the bed where the demon had been. A second later, the Doyen returned.

"Oh, I'm so sorry I left you to deal with things. The demon is dead."

"First it's skin turned a strange color so I quickly disconnected them. It turned to ash as you said it would. Winter has not awoken," said Shea, resisting the urge to flee.

"I'm sure she will awaken by morning. Her body needs time to heal. Are you all right?"

Shea discreetly wiped her hands on the back of her jeans. "Truthfully, I feel exhausted. I think it best if I go to my room now."

The Doyen looked again at the ash on the bed and then back at Shea. For a moment, Shea thought she might not get away with things but then the Doyen smiled. "Please let Isabella know what has transpired before you go to your room. I don't want to leave Winter alone but I think it's best if I left also."

"I will get Isabella for you. Goodnight."

"Goodnight, Shea and thank you again for all you've done tonight. We all must play our part as the Heavens scribe it to be."

With such a cryptic note, Shea finally made her exit. She found Isabella having a heated conversation with Zachary in the kitchen but all stopped once she informed them the demon was dead and the Doyen was leaving. A few minutes later she was finally in her room. For the first hour she paced the room. By the second she was desperate for answers. The only way to get what she wanted meant desperate measures. Using a pair of scissors, she pierced her skin and let the few drops fall into the welcoming fire.

"Ash come to me," said Shea.

A second later swirling smoke engulfed her room. When the form finally solidified Shea gasped.

"Do you not recognize me, sister of my blood?"

Shea's heart raced. The woman standing before her wasn't what she expected. Then again, she'd been condemned to life as a teenager on Earth so what had she thought her twin would look like?

"Sister?" asked Shea.

The woman came closer. She was breathtakingly beautiful. Where Shea had ebony colored hair, the woman had the complete opposite, ivory white with a black stripe down the middle. She smiled but it didn't reach her crystal-clear blue eyes. "Why did you stop talking to me?"

Shea moved closer to the woman. "Oh, sister I never meant for such to happen. It was beyond my control. Something traumatic happened to me and when next I tried to speak to you it wouldn't work. I am so glad Ash found you."

"Yes, your friend found me but he couldn't save me."

"But he did. You are here, which proves it."

The woman turned and then finally sat on Shea's bed. "Do you know what they did to me?"

Shea gently sat next to the woman, her twin. She yearned to hug her but felt a stranger's wall engulf her. She knew nothing of her sister and vice versa. "No. When I was little, I felt this connection to something but it wasn't until I was four when I couldn't finish my supper, I overheard a startling conversation. I heard one of the servants say my sister would get lots of food tonight. It was then I realized I wasn't alone. From that moment on, I ate less and less so you'd have food and I reached out more and more for you. It took a while but finally we did it. We made a connection. Do you remember it?"

The woman stood up quickly. "Your sacrifice was for naught. I never got your food. I was starved all my life. All I knew was pain and misery. I thought I wanted to die but when given the choice, I found a strength I didn't know and said yes to life. Your Ash found me but his father, Lucifer, is the one to have saved me."

Ash, what have I done? Tears pricked Shea's eyes. Did she condemned her sister to a new Hell?

"For the first time since drawing breath I feel powerful. I feel purpose-led. Lucifer was like me–a twin, did you know?"

"No, I didn't."

"Your Heaven isn't so saintly."

"It's your Heaven also," said Shea.

The woman shook her head. "No. Heaven never wanted me. I was a sin. Lucifer explained it all to me. You were born first and thus you are said to have a soul whereas I have none." The woman gave a hurtful laugh.

"It's not my Heaven anymore and I don't believe such. You are a living being and I believe all living things have a soul." said Shea.

The woman looked at her. "Why are you younger?"

Shea quickly explained things. Her twin's anger grew.

"Your Heaven is twisted. They didn't want your help because you were female. Ridiculous. Help is help."

"Not according to the Scriptures which operate as laws in the Heavens."

"So, you've been punished to remain a teenager for eternity?"

Shea got up. The thought she could at some time look like her twin, a full-grown woman, left her feeling angry for the first time with their plight. "For the time being it would appear so. We are hopeful things will change."

"They won't. They don't want it to."

"What is your name by the way?" asked Shea.

"I was called no one but since Lucifer saved me, I've decided to claim the name, Isis, as she was the name of a powerful Egyptian goddess."

"I like your name. Mine is Shea."

"Yes, I know. Ash told me all about you and he made me promise not to kill you."

Shea laughed. Isis did not. "Why would you want to harm me? I am your sister."

"I thought you were the reason for my exile but Lucifer put my thoughts to rest."

"You like Lucifer?"

"You like Ash?" said Isis.

They both smiled.

"Maybe we aren't so dissimilar as we think," said Shea, wondering if such meant the Heavens would never welcome them home.

CHAPTER NINETEEN

"This is the portal you used to get to the place where you found the girl," stated Lucifer, surveying the swirling mass Ash had created.

"I used the same prayer-chant and enchantment so I'm assuming it's the same place."

"Then we must go."

"Father, I can do this. I know how much you don't like to leave your domain."

"For this I will make an exception. I thought once I had burned down this place but I was told a falsehood. Today, I will not make the same mistake."

"It will not be easy. They will now be heavily armed."

Lucifer smiled. Ash's unease grew. "When has easy ever been a demon demand. Come my son, we are wasting time. I will go first and you follow."

Ash nodded. There was no point arguing. Ash watched his father step through the portal and followed. When they landed the landscape had changed. Before it was scaled in grays now it was awash in white. The change was startling. The white gave it an innocent attire, when it was anything but.

Lucifer marched through the swath of snow. "Where is this heavenly army?"

That had been Ash's question. "Trust me they were here."

Lucifer marched unimpeded up to the towering gate.

Ash kicked the door. The sound echoed in the silent landscape. "This doesn't make sense."

Lucifer stilled and Ash got the sense he was using his heightened senses.

"Now it does. There are at least a hundred bodies still living in the building. I believe they were left here to starve and freeze to death. They don't care about them so why bother to fight for them. They think they don't have a soul and therefore are useless."

The truth of his father's words felt like a knife wound. To slowly starve and freeze to death sounded like an order by a cruel master and certainly not one from the Heavens.

"What shall we do?" asked Ash.

"Save them," declared Isis, who strode toward them.

It still stunned Ash, Isis was Shea's twin and more so his father had saved her. She linked arms with Lucifer and then smiled at him.

"Thank you for giving me time with my sister. We still have lots to discuss but she wasn't what I expected. Nor did I kill her."

Ash smiled. "I bet she could say the same."

Isis eyed him. "I see why she likes you. Now time is ticking and we have work to do before we burn it down to ashes, don't we Lucifer."

Lucifer cast a soft look at Isis. "It's far easier to burn it down."

"Why waste flesh. My fellow sisters and brothers will take up arms for you and some might even surprise us with their powers," stated Isis.

Lucifer gave Isis a soft kiss on the lips. "I do like your strategic mind. We take only those with a pulse. Understood."

Ash and Isis nodded and then Lucifer blew the tall imposing door off its hinges like it was made of toothpicks.

Forty minutes later Ash's arms ached and he was sick of snow. He wondered if a demon could get frostbite. He was holding the last young boy in his arms when he heard his father.

"Pick up the pace. I'm going to obliterate this place," said Lucifer.

"I have one last thing to secure," said Ash.

Lucifer took the boy from Ash's arms. "You have five minutes. Then I'm blowing it to Hell." He laughed as he threw the skeletal mass of the youngling through the portal. Ash hoped a demon was there to catch him.

Ash didn't respond to his father. He dashed back to the place. As he'd secured the angels from the place, he'd been surprised to discover a stack of books in the basement. Knowledge was key and he wondered why ancient books would be in the building. What better place to hide knowledge? Armed with newfound strength, Ash didn't waste time. He darted into the cellar in the basement with the books, scooped the three ancient tomes up in his arms and ran through the maze of corridors, hoping his father was feeling lenient with time.

The second his feet crossed the blown-apart door, his father's wrath rained down on the place. Ash ran faster to avoid the falling debris. He reached the portal before his father saw what was in his arms and thankfully made it through and into his room before being once again summoned.

"Ash, your sister is still healing from her recent wounds. For the time being, I've appointed Isis to the healing of her sisters and brethren. Ninety-three made it and I will use them to get what I want," said Lucifer. "Once they are ready, your job will be to train them to fight. I need every demon I can get if I'm going to take over the Heavens."

A statement echoed by Isabella, thought Ash. He nodded and then quickly departed. The longing to see Shea burned within him. Turning to smoke, he rematerialized in Shea's room.

CHAPTER TWENTY

Isabella didn't like surprises. Lately, they were toppling her in what some would cite as miraculous ways. Izzy wasn't convinced in their heavenly grace.

Winter was alive. The demon blood transplant had worked. She should be rejoicing, like her fellow sisters. But she felt off. Meredith would advise her to work out, or give into Nathanael, who wanted them to establish some sort of "formal" relationship. Her heart and most certainly her body yearned to take the easy road, but she would not abandon her fallen sisters.

"Why are you brooding?" asked Meredith.

"I can't explain it but I..."

"Feel off," finished Meredith, claiming the other chair in Izzy's office.

Izzy nodded.

"I think what we need is to sing," said Meredith, stunning Izzy.

They hadn't sung as a band since the night Nathanael had shown up to throw their world into chaos. However, the idea wasn't without merit. As a band they were united, strong and focused. When they sung, their voice soothed those in need and also helped to recharge them.

Izzy got up from her chair. "I think you're right. Get Mike to set-up a gig for us for a week's time and tell the sisters we're going to practice tonight at seven."

"Wonderful. Anya would like to join us and she mentioned she found an old song in one of the books she's been reading which she thought would be good for the band."

"An old song? How old?"

"Honestly, I have no idea. You could talk to her about it, or wait for tonight."

"I'll wait for tonight. I think I'm going to go out for a run."

"It's freezing outside. They said it's fourteen degrees Fahrenheit and will be even colder. They say we're getting a huge blizzard."

Izzy smiled. She hated the cold but the pain would do her good. "I will be fine. Would you like to join me?"

Meredith laughed. "It's a kind offer but I must humbly refuse. While Winter is on the mend, I do have a number of things I've put off which I must attended to."

"Speaking of attending to, how are things between you and Zachary?"

"We are managing."

"I think you two are avoiding each other," said Izzy.

"The same could be said of you. Why not invite Nathanael to join you on your delightful winter day run?"

"He does not like the cold."

"He would for you," said Meredith, smiling.

"Meredith, relationships are puzzles and while I am enjoying getting to know more of Nathanael, I do not want to give up my independence."

Meredith nodded. "I do understand you, Izzy. It's times like these, I wish our mothers were alive."

Izzy sighed. "I've been thinking of our mothers of late. They made their relationships seem blissful but now I wonder if my perception of things, from the eyes of a child was naive."

"I do not know. My mother seemed happy but then she didn't question things."

Izzy laughed. "She certainly questioned the Oracle who came with orders from the Holy Waters on the day announcing you were to be Zachary's wife."

Meredith stood up. "I had forgotten. You are correct. I remember being surprised by her reaction, but then..."

"Then your father came in the room and all discussion stopped."

Meredith nodded. "My mother would never question him but I believe more than anything she was surprised I, her daughter, would be chosen for the mighty Zachary."

"If only she could see you know. I do believe she'd be proud of you," said Izzy.

"I'm not sure she'd agree as she gave her soul to the traditional teachings, but I have no regrets."

Izzy looked at her best friend for a moment. "We all have regrets, Meredith, but we also have all changed. We are not the angels we were when our home was the Heavens. I believe we are stronger and better."

Meredith smiled. "You are correct plus you're going to need all your strength for the run you're planning to enjoy."

"Are you sure I can't convince you to join me?"

Meredith stopped at the office door. "Maybe, on the day Hell freezes over but until then, the cold and I are not friends."

"You are tougher than you think, Meredith."

"And you, Izzy are still as stubborn as I remember. I'm going to let the sisters know about our plans for the band and practice tonight. Enjoy your run," said Meredith, as she exited the room.

Izzy smiled as she made her way to her bedroom to change from her prayer robe into running attire. She too hated the cold but having lived a life bent on sacrifice, she oddly looked forward to the lashing sting of the bitter weather on her skin.

CHAPTER TWENTY-ONE

S hea hadn't sung since the incident. When Meredith had informed her the band, known as Minstrel Singers, was getting back together for a gig, she thought the idea of bringing forth her voice would terrify her. It was not the case. She stood on the stage to practice with her sisters surrounding her, and felt empowered. The song was ancient, the knowledge was baked into the marrow of her bones and she liked the feel of power as she recited the rhythmic archaic words. She let the flow of the words siphon through her and was totally lost in the melody. It took her a few seconds to realize her voice was the only one echoing in the room.

"Oh, sorry," she said.

Anya, the sister to her right, reached out and gave her hand a squeeze. "I had forgotten how much I enjoy listening to your voice."

"As had I," said Meredith, smiling.

"Shea, you should take the lead on this song," said Isabella, surprising her.

Shea immediately tried to slink back but Anya gave her a coy smile and tightened her grip. "Oh, I don't think so."

Isabella moved from center stage to where Shea stood. "Yes, you must. This song is about resurrection and it suits you."

Shea heard the collective gasps from her sisters and her heart shuddered. Isabella, their leader, had for once voiced their private thoughts. Shea would never be the same.

"What Isabella is trying to say is you have strength in your voice and the ancient words seem best suited to you taking the lead. We will be with you, as always, but we also don't want to pressure you," said Meredith, who was collecting the song sheets.

"Yes, we do," stated Isabella, cocking her head at Shea.

"Isabella, she might not be ready," said Meredith, coming to her rescue.

"It's too much pressure," said another sister.

Shea finally let go of Anya's hand. "I'll do it," she said, surprising herself.

"Are you sure?" asked Meredith, who was still looking at Isabella.

"She said she'd do it. It's settled," said Isabella, giving Shea a wink.

Shea smiled. She could do it and she would.

Mike walked into the room and ushered over Isabella. Meredith gave them a few more instructions specific to the set and then Shea and the rest of her sisters were finally free. They were almost at the door when Isabella halted everyone.

"Well, it seems there's been a change of plans. The gig is now set for tomorrow tonight and it's at the Ritz-Carleton and we're part of the Jewish Young Professionals Bash. Seems we're the closing act. Mike's arranged for our drives to and from the place so we'll meet back here at six."

"What should we wear?" asked Anya.

Isabella seemed to think about it. "We'll wear what we normally do. I'm not changing our uniforms for this one night."

Mike said something quietly to her and Isabella brushed him off. "Again, six o'clock here tomorrow night. You still up to what we discussed earlier, Shea?"

Nervous flutters flitted in her stomach but Shea turned to look directly at Isabella. "Yes. I'm still good."

Isabella graced her with a stunning smile. "I know you'll do us proud."

Shea realized something. She didn't care about making them proud. She had to do this for herself. Ash had taken so much from her she'd wondered if her voice too had been claimed by him. Knowing what she knew now, she smiled as she opened her bedroom door, not one bit surprised to see her demon lounging by the fire roaring in her room.

"Now, that I like to see," said Ash, moving to greet her.

Since Shea had invited him once into their house, he'd explained he could easily visit her. Had Shea truly understood the extent of her invitation, she wasn't sure she would have invited him in the first place.

Dressed in his handsome teenage guise, he truly was a sight to behold. Leather pants clung to him and power resonated from every chiseled feature he wore with ease.

"I head you and your sister had a good conversation," said Ash, gently taking her hand to lead her toward the heat from the fire.

Shea shivered. She'd been cold in the practice room but had ignored it. Now she held out her hands for much-needed warmth. "She wasn't what I expected."

It took Ash a few seconds before he responded. "I am sorry. Are you okay with it?"

Shea rolled her eyes, making him laugh. "I have no choice. What's to be has been done and written."

"At least we saved her and the others."

"The others?"

"We went back and rescued as many as we could."

Shea felt herself reaching out to Ash. "You saved them?"

Ash pulled her closer to his form, his warm arms adding a layer of heat that sizzled her toes. "Yes, we did."

"Who exactly is this we?"

"My father and your sister. Actually, it was your twin's idea to save them and my father seems oddly taken with her, so he complied. Then in more Lucifer fashion he burned the place to the ground."

"Of such, I am grateful. So, where are they?"

Ash slowly pulled away. "In Hell."

"What do you mean, in Hell?"

"Your twin suggested once they are healthy, Lucifer could train them and add them to his army. My father thought it a splendid idea."

"I'm sorry, I don't understand. I thought angels couldn't be in Hell?"

"Well, technically true, but if they have a bit of demon blood running in their veins it's not an issue."

Shea eased completely out of his hold. She squatted down to get closer to the fire. "Let me see if I understand. An angel can descend to the Hell realm if they are tainted with demon blood."

"Yes, correct."

"So, is it the same for Heaven?"

Ash knelt beside her. He held out his too-beautiful hands and the flames eagerly leaped for his attentions. "I've never thought about it but maybe."

Shea stood; she needed distance from Ash. He scattered her thoughts. "So, I can descend to your realm."

Ash closed the small space between them. Shea found herself pinned to the wall. The hard wood dug in her back and Ash blanketed his front. "Taking you to my realm is impossible."

Shea tilted her head back. "Why?"

His lips lowered until they were a breath from sealing hers. "Because you are my treasure."

Shea thought to demand more but obviously his patience had run out. His lips when they did finally claim her, allowed her anger to rise. She knew he'd be gentle but she was done playing his game. Shea arched her back and plunged her hands into his thick hair. He kissed like an expert, something she didn't want. She needed him hot and wild. Boldly, Shea bit his lips and the taste of his blood on her tongue caused her to groan. His arms lashed her to him. His grip was punishing.

"Shea," he said, his voice sounding like a heavenly grace.

"Ash," she said, racking her fingers down his spine.

He gently lifted his head to look at her. "You sure about this?"

The fact he asked, was granting her the right to set the limit when she knew his control was barely tethered made her smile. She licked her lips and took delight in the heat in his eyes as he followed her actions.

"We've done this before, haven't we?"

He gasped. "I took your memories to spare you."

"When I awoke alone in that alley I thought something else had happened. But, I remember. I'm not ashamed. You asked me then, if I recall?"

"Well, yes of course but I admit you bedazzled me."

Shea let her hand gently stroke through his hair. "I bedazzled you?"

"The minute I saw you, I knew you were mine and it terrified me. How was I to make you see our destiny was linked?"

Shea reached under his shirt and ran her hand along his chest. "You gave me the choice then and I accepted. I'm ready for more."

Ash chuckled. "Are you sure?"

"Why is everyone second-guessing my choices? I know what I want and I want you."

Ash scooped her into his arms and eased her onto her bed. "I'm all yours for the taking," he said.

Why waste their time with words, thought Shea as she quickly divested him of his clothes. He laid on her bed like a sacrifice. Awaiting her judging eyes, she sensed his vulnerability. Actions certainly had more merit, thought Shea, as she stood and just as fast removed her own clothing. They didn't need a blanket for warmth. The minute they were skin-to-skin, heat the likes of which Shea had thought had been once a dream, and now a realized memory, caused her to sigh in bliss. This was exactly what she craved.

Sinning never felt so heavenly good, thought Shea, ignoring the old adage that too much pleasure wasn't a good thing.

CHAPTER TWENTY-TWO

"How are you feeling, Winter?" asked Meredith. It was her turn to sit with Winter to ensure the earth-born angel was healing. She'd always found it hard to spend time sitting and talking but since she'd discovered more about the origins of the earth-born angels she'd vowed to do a little digging. The thought Sky or Winter could have committed grievous crimes to become such wasn't something she could reconcile.

"I am getting better. Do you think I'll be able to go home today?"

Meredith knew Winter was well enough to go home, but Izzy wanted answers. If Meredith couldn't pry some knowledge from her, Izzy would steal it from her. Izzy's talent, more a curse thought Meredith, was her ability to touch anyone and see their history. When Izzy did touch skin-to-skin the toil it took on her was harsh. If Meredith could spare her best friend, she would, hence why she was sitting and talking to Winter.

"I think you'll be able to leave either today or tomorrow. I brought you a chai latte, the type you like."

Winter smiled. "Oh, you shouldn't have, but thank you."

Meredith handed the drink to Winter, who propped herself up to a sitting position on the bed. She took a tentative sip and smiled.

"Thank you, this is lovely and just like I like it. Your chef is amazing."

Meredith laughed. "Well, I confess this chef was Starbucks, located around the corner. I asked Sky what you liked and she told me."

Winter laughed. The sound, beautiful, filled the small bedroom. It was a harsh reminder of how dark the room had been days ago when she had been on the brink of death.

"Do you remember anything about the night you were injured?"

Winter nodded. "A little. I remember Gareth fighting with a female demon and the next thing I knew I felt a piercing pain and then everything went cold and dark. It felt..."

"Yes, it felt like what, Winter?"

Winter took another sip of her latte. Meredith sensed she was gathering her courage.

"It felt like death."

Meredith gasped. "You died before?"

Another nod from Winter, who couldn't quite look Meredith in the eye.

Winter turned her face to the window. The sun was starting to set. Meredith knew tomorrow she'd be on the stage with her other sisters singing their souls out to a packed house. If she thought of it she'd get nervous. She focused on her young charge.

Winter's long mahogany hair was today braided, hanging down her back. She had pretty blue feather earrings dangling on her ears. Her skin, tan-colored, was looking once again healthy. Winter wasn't tiny. She was close to six feet, long-limbed but lithe and graceful on her feet. She had eyes the color of chocolate and a tiny nose with high cheekbones. Meredith had never before wondered about her earth-born heritage but today she did.

"Winter, I know nothing about you or your sister, Sky, but I'd like to. Would you tell me about yourself and how you came to be an earth-born angel?" asked Meredith.

"My Doyen told me you'd ask. I had hoped you wouldn't. It's not a happy story."

"I don't want to pry."

"Yes, Meredith you do. I get it. We deceived you. We pretended to not know how to fight and we thought your tale of a demon army false. It was wrong of us. We are sorry. We should have trusted each other. I am sorry."

Meredith was stunned. She sat back in her chair. Winter's tone and everything about her radiated a wise energy, one she never showcased before.

"Where to start," said Winter.

"I usually find the beginning to be a good place."

She gave a small heartful laugh. "My beginning isn't easy. My mother was a Chappaquiddick Wampanoag Indian who fell in love with the wrong man. Story of her life, or maybe the story of the majority of women's lives. Anyway, she left her family and followed him to the city. She had me a year later and my sister was born less than a year after me. With two small children she couldn't work and my father liked to drink. He could barely keep a job and we had to keep moving for him to find employment. By the time I was ten we had moved to five different cities. By the time I was twelve I learned to keep myself and my sister quiet to avoid my father. My parents fought all the time. My mother tried to get a job but she was Indian with no skills and the color of her skin made her an outcast. We were lucky if she could get work washing clothes or cooking for a family. My mother got sick when I was fifteen and died within six months. Less than a year later my father raped me."

Meredith felt bile rise up and knew she couldn't mask her facial reaction.

"I'm so sorry, Winter."

"It was a long time ago. I've detached myself from this history, but you asked to hear it."

"I did. I'm sorry."

Winter finished her latte and set the cup on the side table.

"When my father tried to rape my sister, I killed him."

It took Meredith a moment to truly absorb Winter's confession.

"I'm sure it was an accident," said Meredith, automatically.

Winter turned and pinned Meredith with a cold stare.

"No, Meredith it wasn't. I knew exactly what I was doing. I had planned it in my head. I vowed, I wouldn't let anyone hurt my sister and I'm not sorry for my actions. I paid the price in the end and kept my vow to my sister. She lived a happy life."

Again, Meredith absorbed her words. Her sister had lived a healthy life. "How old are you, Winter?"

Winter smiled. In no ways did it reach her eyes. "I've lost count. I believe at least 170. I stopped aging the day I died."

Winter looked like a teenager. "How did you die?"

"I was hanged for murdering my father."

Meredith gasped. She knew human history had been harsh but hearing a first-hand account of it felt brutally raw.

"And your sister, dare I ask what happened to her?"

"Before our mother died she told me of our people. I found a lady in our area who knew of my mother's people and she promise me she'd ensure my sister was safely returned to our people. For months I scrapped and stole what I could get my hands on and I left her all my savings.

She escaped and reclaimed her heritage and I am proud of her."

"Oh, Winter, your mother would be proud of you."

"I know she would. I don't regret the choice I made and I'd do it again but I do miss my people."

"You can't go back?"

It wasn't a question. Meredith knew the answer. Winter was like her, exiled and shunned by their own families.

"I went back once in those early years as I adjusted to ensure my sister was okay and it was enough for me."

"Did you speak to her?"

"No. That wouldn't have worked. I'm the walking dead to her. What I do now, is right wrongs. I never felt powerful growing up but I do now."

Meredith got up from her chair. "I get it. We are not so different."

Winter laughed as she hauled the blanket tighter around her. "I highly suspect you haven't killed anyone."

Meredith looked out the window. Yes, she'd killed demons but she'd also killed her way of life, her chance at love and all hopes for her family. Did she kill like Winter had? No. That didn't mean she didn't understand Winter's actions. Deep down, Meredith applauded Winter's bravery. She stood up for her sister and herself and while Winter spoke in succinct sentences, Meredith sensed she still warred with her actions.

"No, I haven't killed a human, but I've certainly killed demons. It sounds to me like your father, was a demon."

"If only it were that simple. My father was a sick man and this world has lots of sick men."

"I get now why when Lilith came to you with the offer of life you took it."

"Lilith didn't offer me life, Meredith."

"What?"

"I wasn't interested in life. She knew my true desire. Lilith offered me power and a chance to change the world, plus immortality. When I accepted, I didn't realize exactly what it all meant."

"Yes, it's the fine print we always seem to miss."

"Like you, I'm resigned to the guise of a teenager. The same for Sky. It's certainly not easy. We don't fit in but yet we do. Teenagers live on the outskirts no matter what century were in. Thank you again for saving me."

Meredith walked back to Winter's bed and took her hand. "It was the least we could do. Thank you, Winter for telling me your story. I think since truths have been spoken we will grow closer. Your Doyen is working with Izzy now and we need all the help we can get if we're to defeat Lucifer's demon army which he's amassing to invade the Heavens."

Winter sighed. "I fear it won't be enough."

Meredith gave her an assessing look. "Our faith will sustain us and we must try."

"I agree with you, but our numbers won't be enough. We need to convert more to our cause."

The sentiment was exactly what Meredith had been discussing with Izzy. "I agree with you but at the moment recruitment isn't possible."

Winter sat up in the bed. "You are singing tomorrow, correct?"

"Yes."

"Have you thought of using your voice to recruit others?"

Meredith laughed and then when she saw Winter was dead serious she frowned. "Winter, we can't recruit humans for this fight."

"I know my suggestion might seem ludicrous but talk to the devoted and once you have befriended some you might be surprised to discover they'd be willing to fight."

What Winter said made sense but it would also put them all at risk. "I will think about it. I worry..."

"You worry you'll be putting your fellow sisters at risk. Talk to the Doyen and if she agrees with my idea ask her to hold a meeting at the house for those who seem interested."

Meredith nodded. "Thank you, Winter for your suggestion. Now, you must rest. I'm going to leave you to sleep but I truly appreciate your honesty and suggestions."

Winter settled back under the blankets. "Thank you, Meredith for saving me."

Meredith walked to the door and chuckled. "Seems to me you're thinking of ways to save us all."

Winter closed her eyes and Meredith quietly vacated the room. Once again the earth-born angel had surprised her.

"It is good to see you smiling, Meredith," said Zachary.

The smile quickly left Meredith's face. She hadn't sensed Zachary and had thought he'd still be in the training room.

Zachary came closer. "You are avoiding me."

Meredith had but she wasn't about to admit it, and what did he expect? "I have been busy."

"Winter is healing well," stated Zachary, assuming all was well.

His smugness is what ignited her anger. "No thanks to you."

Zachary stiffened. "I would have offered to sing but I am sure your fellow sisters would not have appreciated my hidden talents."

Meredith stopped walking and then she couldn't help it; she burst out laughing. "I am sorry, Zachary but do you even sing?"

"I have been known to sing in the shower."

Okay, that image wasn't one she wanted to dwell on. "Well, in this case we're lucky. Winter has made a full recovery and we will save your voice for another crisis. I was heading to the kitchen. I heard cinnamon buns were in the works and I confess to craving one. Please join me."

Zachary moved to her side and held out his arm, indicting he'd guide her to the kitchen.

"It would be my honor to join you and I too confess to enjoying the sweetness of cinnamon buns. I am discovering Earth is not like I remember."

Meredith looked at Zachary. She'd forgotten he had his own unique history with Earth and humans and it was a subtle reminder he was a lot older than her.

"It took me a long time to adapt to Earth and to human ways."

"Faith, I have discovered is still a test for humans. Many years ago, when I walked this Earth, I was steadfast in my belief humans did not merit the Almighty's grace. Time is still testing humans but they have accomplished more than I thought," said Zachary as they both slipped into the warm kitchen.

"Well, did the Heavens flood? This is a sight I never thought to see–the two of you getting along like old times," said Izzy, licking her fingers as she polished off the final piece of her cinnamon bun.

Meredith quickly retracted her arm and ignored Izzy's comment. "We came for the sugar high."

"You and everyone else. They are delicious. How did your time with Winter go?" asked Izzy, pulling up a stool for Meredith to sit on.

With the roles reversed, it was Zachary who dished her out a cinnamon bun. "Thank you, Zachary. Winter had some interesting ideas."

"About what?" asked Izzy, taking a drink of water.

Meredith took a bite of the still-warm bun and savored the moist but sugary delight. "She expressed what we talked about. We don't have the numbers and need to recruit more. She suggested we recruit humans."

"Humans?" asked Izzy, looking perplexed.

"There will be no recruitment of humans," said Zachary, who took a huge bite of the bun.

"It was an idea I find hard to agree with but we might not have a choice," said Meredith.

"Meredith, there is always a choice. Some are the right choices and others wrong," said Zachary.

Is he talking about teaching us to fight or the current situation we're in? wondered Meredith.

"At this time, I agree with you, Zachary. Humans don't believe in angels and if they were to see one they would think we can grant miracles. I have seen enough of their strange television shows to know the reality they face is not something they could handle. I can't see how recruiting humans to our cause would help. In all likelihood they would impede our training and chances at stopping Lucifer's army."

Meredith and Zachary nodded in affirmation. Meredith had a flashback to a time when Zachary had first started to teach them to fight in the Heavens. They'd finished a week's worth of training and the three of them had enjoyed a lovely meal on the meadows. Izzy had been the first to leave and then it had been the two of them. She and Zachary had talked for hours. She'd been young and naive and had thought then they could be together some day.

The Oracle said she was to be his b'iã but within a few months she'd lost everything–her heavenly home, Zachary and her chance for a family of her own to love. As Meredith digested the bun and the remnants of the memories, she realized she'd gained things also–independence, a sense of self-worth, the ability to hold her own against a demon, and most importantly she did have a home. Here, in this brownstone, she had her sisters; a family of sorts. She wasn't sorry for what she'd sacrificed to get where she was today. She couldn't change the past but Meredith vowed she'd be the one steering her future. If she had a home, she might find a way to have a family. It had been her nightly prayer since being exiled.

"Do you smell smoke?" asked Zachary.

The three of them looked around the cozy kitchen, which was fire free. A second later a loud fire alarm screeched throughout the house. As they darted from the kitchen to find the source of the fire, Meredith wondered if she might lose the house she'd called home for over a decade.

CHAPTER TWENTY-THREE

For a moment when Shea had smelled smoke she'd wondered if it had originated from her and Ash. The thought terrified her.

"You are in danger," said Ash, moving with grace from the bed.

Shea dressed quickly. "You must leave."

"I will not leave until you are safe and trust me when there's smoke there's fire."

Smoke curled under her door and Shea tried hard to suppress a cough but failed.

"Stay here. I'm going to scope out what's happening."

It was on the tip of Shea's tongue to say, "be careful" but he disappeared in a blink. Shea looked out the window. She was on the top floor of the brownstone and unfortunately her window faced the street. It was daylight and already her fellow sisters were streaming out of the house while nearby pedestrians gathered close. If she jumped, it would be without her wings which meant the fall to the ground would kill her. If she stayed, she worried the fire would consume her.

The flames in her fireplace leaped to life.

"Shea, take my hand."

The voice wasn't Ash's. Shea opened the door instead of moving toward the fireplace. Smoke slammed into her and she closed her eyes to maneuver down the stairs. She didn't see fire, but eerie green-colored smoke curled around her. Shea started coughing and then she couldn't breathe. She stumbled on a step and the next thing she felt were Ash's hands catching her.

"Why is it, my b'iã, you never listen to instructions?"

Shea yearned to answer but her lungs wouldn't obey.

"Hush, I have you," said Ash and then before Shea could question his actions, she felt a strange sensation as space and time dissolved.

When next Shea opened her eyes, she was in the back alley, away from prying eyes.

"I am here, Shea," said Ash, and while Shea couldn't see him she felt his arms around her.

"I must go back. There are more of your sisters trapped inside."

"Save them."

"I do this for you because their passing would make you sad and I can't abide anything but your happiness. I wonder what they will think with a demon saving them?"

"Be safe," said Shea, this time, before the warmth of his arms dissolved. Finally, alone and able to catch her breath, Shea ran to the front of the brownstone.

"Oh, Shea thank the Heavens you are safe," said Meredith.

"Who is still in the house?"

"We're not sure. Izzy ran back inside with Nathanael to ensure Winter and Anya had made it out."

The shrill shrieks of the fire trucks stopped their conservation. A few seconds later, Izzy ran out with Nathanael who had Anya over his shoulder.

"Where is Winter?" asked Meredith.

"We searched for her but she must have left. The house is empty. It's strange too. There's lots of weird green-colored smoke but we couldn't find the fire."

"I am sure the firemen will do their job. I am praying we will have a roof over our heads tonight," said Meredith.

"Is everyone out?" asked a fireman.

Izzy immediately told him she thought so and explained they couldn't find the fire. The fireman moved everyone back further off the sidewalk. A gust of wind swept past everyone as it entered the house. Half an hour later the fireman had cleared the house of any fire and the wind had cleaned out the smoke in the house.

"Strangest fire I've ever seen," said one of the firemen, as he rolled-up his hose.

"Thank you. Is it safe for us to return to the house?" asked Izzy.

"Yes, but keep your eyes open and if smoke materializes again don't hesitate to call us," said the Captain of the local fire department, handing Izzy his business card. Only once the two fire trucks had left did Meredith and Shea turn toward the front of the brownstone.

"Would figure," said Meredith.

Shea knew instantly whom she referenced. There standing on their front door stoop was Zachary.

"Dare we thank thee for the blessed wind?" asked Meredith as she walked toward him.

He smiled. "Well, I wasn't about to let your house be consumed by fire."

"I was told there was no fire," said Izzy, walking past Zachary to inspect the inside.

"Thank you," said Shea, keeping her eyes downcast.

"Yes, thank you. The thought of being homeless again... well, I'm certainly saying a prayer of thanks," said Meredith as she gingerly went back inside the brownstone.

"Are thee well?" asked Zachary to Shea as she attempted to walk past him.

Shea had never been addressed ever by the mighty Seraphim warrior and was momentarily stunned. Gathering her composure, she mustered her strength to answer.

"I am unharmed."

"But you are burned," declared Zachary, halting Meredith's inside investigation.

Shea immediately tugged her sweater lower to cover her wrists. "I am fine." Not wanting to call attention to herself, she darted past Zachary and Meredith to the stairs. Only once she had closed her bedroom door did she breathe easy.

"Shea, we have a slight problem," said Ash, materializing in solid form.

Why did this news not surprise her.

"And it would be?"

"My sister took Winter."

Okay, that hadn't been what she'd expected but it could be worse.

"And..."

Ash sat on her bed looking confused and lost. Feeling the need to be close to him, she sat next to him. "And what?"

"Well, this I didn't see coming."

"What would that be?"

"Your sister married my father. She is now the Queen of Hell."

Okay, that most certainly wasn't a slight problem at all. It was one devilish nightmare neither of them had anticipated and not good for any of them. Most importantly it meant the secret Shea had kept sealed tight from her fellow sisters might have to be unsealed. That more than thinking of her twin as the Queen of Hell, worried Shea.

CHAPTER TWENTY-FOUR

Something was at play but Meredith couldn't put her finger on it. She hadn't seen Gareth in days, which was highly unusual.

"Meredith, a moment," said Zachary, with a nod of his head.

Meredith didn't want to give him a moment. She wanted to thoroughly check the house. Smoke without fire didn't seem right. He didn't even look over his shoulder to see if she followed him into the dining room, he assumed. His assumption grated on her.

She stepped into the room, wondering why it smelled like a freshly-lit candle instead of the grime of smoke. She surveyed the walls and realized none were charred with smoke. "Yes," she said, hating that she'd obeyed.

"Shea smells of demon," stated Zachary.

Meredith gave him an incredulous look. Then it dawned on her, he might not know what had happened to her fellow sister.

"Zachary, she was assaulted."

"I know of her history but when she passed me a moment ago she reeked of demon. Trust me, I know."

"You are saying this is something new?"

He nodded. "I think you need to watch her."

"Watch her? You say it like I shouldn't trust her."

"Exactly. Something is afoot here. Smoke without fire is a demon ruse as old as time. What do you know of the night she fell?"

It was on the tip of Meredith's tongue to scream at him. We fell a long time ago. Meredith thought back to the night which changed things. Much at the time had seemed surreal. They'd found Shea unconscious in a dark alley close to morning. It had been obvious she'd been assaulted with cuts on her arms, a bruised face and ... Meredith didn't want to visualize how her body had been on display, clearly indicating she'd been raped.

"Trust me, what befell Shea almost killed her."

Zachary moved to the window to observe the street. "But it didn't."

"And for such we are blessed. My fellow sisters and I, we are grateful. What are you not telling me?"

He turned to give her a penetrating look. "Did none of you think it odd she hadn't been killed?"

He'd nailed the one thought both she and Izzy had talked about. Why leave Shea alive when demons were not known for mercy.

"At the time, both Izzy and I thought it miraculous. Morning light had begun to stream and we assumed the blessed light was what forced the demons to flee and kept her alive in time for us to find her and bring her back here and heal her. You can't imagine this was a falsehood she created."

"I don't believe she created the falsehood but I'm beginning to think someone is orchestrating things here."

"The smoke? You think a demon was here? If so, for what purpose?"

"I don't know but more importantly, I do want you to watch Shea and report to me. I must leave you for a while and..."

Meredith gnashed her teeth together. She most certainly would not report to Zachary.

"And?"

"I have a duty to attend to in the heavenly realm. I don't expect to be long."

"Zachary what you do with your time is your time. In case you missed it, we got along fine without your presence before and we can take care of ourselves."

He moved to stand next to her. There was an odd light, almost a twinkle in his eyes, which should have warned Meredith something was up.

"I have no desire to leave you."

"Again, we'll be fine," said Meredith.

He gently cupped her chin which tilted her face up. The move shocked Meredith to the core. He was Seraphim, she a fallen angel, yet he was touching her.

"I understand now what my actions did and I am sorry."

Sorry? Did Hell freeze over? The mighty Zachary said sorry. This was becoming the strangest of days, thought Meredith.

"We are okay."

"You are more than fine. Now, I understand why my hands were tied. I wanted to speak in all of your defense at the Council but alas I had made a vow and...I see now this is how the divinity of the Almighty works."

Zachary leaned closer to her. His lips an inch from her face. Meredith's world stopped.

"When I return we will have a much-needed candid talk but know in my heart you are my chosen."

"I...I...what?" sputtered Meredith, a second before the all-mighty Zachary kissed her, the touch as soft as newborn angel's wings.

When he released her, Meredith stood still.

"Keep an eye on Shea and I will see you soon," said Zachary, strolling out of the room like what he'd done to her senses and her heart was an ordinary occurrence.

"Meredith, what did Zachary want?" asked Izzy, marching into the dining room.

Meredith swallowed and forced her heart to a steady beat. "He's worried about Shea." A truism of sorts, but what worried Meredith more was her reaction. She'd steeled herself years ago that the lure of Zachary would not be, and she'd survived with her coating of armor as her shield. Now, the shield felt heavy and she worried letting it go would truly destroy her.

"Shea? How dare he. She's been through so much."

Izzy did have a point. "How is the rest of the house?"

"Perfectly fine. Not a scratch of soot or lingering odor. I don't like it."

"Zachary thinks a demon was in our house."

Izzy paced like a caged lion in the dining room. "I agree. I spoke with Nathanael and we feel we've been breached."

"But to what end? We're all okay."

"I've asked Mike to call the Doyen to ensure Winter is okay. The thought of a demon in our house makes me angry. We have safety measures in place. How could this happen and why? Why smoke us out and not simply burn our house to the ground and try to kill us?"

"It is daytime," spoke Meredith.

Izzy stopped pacing. "Ah, I hadn't thought of that. Maybe..."

Mike ran into the house shouting for Izzy.

"In here, Mike," said Izzy, ushering him into the room.

"The Doyen said Winter never made it to the safehouse and she can't sense her."

"You don't think the demon took Winter?" asked Meredith, trying to sort through what was going on.

"It's exactly what I think," said Izzy.

"But why?" asked Mike.

A second later another commotion at the door had all three of them running into the hall.

There, barely standing was one gaunt looking Gareth.

Meredith rushed to his side; fearful he was about to collapse. "Gareth, what happened?"

"What day is it?" he managed to croak as he slid to the wooden floor in the hall.

Mike said, "Thursday."

"The date," whispered Gareth.

When Izzy told him the date he gasped.

"What is it, Gareth?" asked Izzy, coming to kneel next to him.

"I've been gone over two weeks," he said, with a haunted look.

"Don't be ridiculous. We saw you two days ago," said Mike.

Gareth shook his head. "It wasn't me. I've been...this is going to sound weird but I woke up a block from here in a deserted building and my last thought was I was talking with this guy in the alley and then everything went black. I have strange memories. Something happened to me."

Meredith and Izzy exchanged a look.

"We will find out what happened but for now you need to rest. Mike, help Meredith take him to the guest room to rest. I will have Nayla make something healthy for you to eat. You look like..."

"Not like the Gareth we saw in training two days ago," said Mike, helping to haul Gareth to his feet.

Meredith and Mike maneuvered Gareth into the guest room on the second floor. He no sooner hit the bed than he fell asleep.

"He's exhausted," stated Meredith.

"What's going on?" asked Mike.

Izzy came into the room, bearing four purple candles. She handed two to Meredith. "We are being played."

Mike watched as they lit a purple candle in each corner of the room. "Played by who?"

"I fear a demon," said Meredith, taking Izzy's hand.

Mike knew enough to remain silent as Meredith and Izzy spoke as one in an ancient heavenly language he felt to the marrow of his bones. He knew they were placing a protective barrier around the room. While the candles would help bring safety to the room, he worried about them.

"You're saying a demon took Gareth," said Mike, trying to comprehend things.

"Worse," said Meredith.

"How so?" asked Mike.

"A demon possessed Gareth and he was able to breach our heavenly-fortified house."

"As horrible as it is, the bigger question remains why and in all that time, why not kill us?" asked Izzy.

"Maybe the demon wanted intel," said Mike, as they moved out of the room and closed the door so Gareth could rest.

"Well, the demon is certainly armed with our intel now," said Izzy, all but running down the stairs.

"Where are you going?" asked Meredith.

Izzy stopped with her hand on the doorknob. "I need to have a talk with the Doyen. We need to find Winter."

"What should we do?" asked Meredith, a shiver of fear skating through her. First the smoke, then Zachary's accusations about Shea and now knowing Gareth had been possessed made her realize they truly weren't safe.

"Watch Gareth and watch Shea," said Izzy, exiting the house before Mike or Meredith could ask more questions.

"What's wrong with Shea?" asked Mike, following Meredith into the kitchen.

"Hopefully nothing."

"You don't think after all she endured and went through she's involved in what's happening," said Mike, sounding as she had earlier; incredulous.

Meredith put the kettle on. She need a hot chocolate to calm her nerves. By the blessed light, I'm acting like your average teenager, she thought, willing the water to boil as she dished out two heaping spoonful's of cocoa in her favorite mug. Mike took a mug and added a teabag to his.

"I need to pray," said Meredith. She was an angel who had been honed to fight and one who didn't flee when demons came at her. The thought of a demon orchestrating all that had transpired made her feel sick. Thinking her fellow sister, Shea, could somehow be wrapped up in all of this made her want to smash something. Shea would give her life for any one of them, reminded Meredith. She left Mike to his tea as she made her way to the prayer room, taking a sip of the still-too-hot beverage, trying with all her heart to believe her reasoning.

Shea would never deceive them, thought Meredith. She shuddered, realizing doubt could be as strong as a heavenly sword. Finishing her beverage, Meredith got on her knees. She prayed for guidance and strength, all the while trying to ignore the doubt tugging at her subconscious and the hope making her recall the feel of Zachary's lips.

CHAPTER TWENTY-FIVE

Izzy ran like the hounds of Hell were nipping at her heels. She knew she was a sight as humans cast her a disturbing look as she darted down the busy sidewalk but she didn't care. She didn't need to knock on the large mahogany door of the Earth-angels safe house. The Doyen, herself, opened it.

"Has Winter shown up?" asked Izzy, darting inside and daring to take a breath.

The Doyen walked past her and led Izzy into the prayer room. "No. I don't sense her in this realm."

For a second, Izzy faltered. She sensed there was something unsaid. "Do you sense her in any other realm?"

A slit of a smile filtered quickly across the Doyen's face. "Yes."

"Where?"

"In Hell."

"Nice gift bequeathed to thee," said Izzy, realizing the significance of what she'd discerned. The Doyen had been made by Lilith, who was tied to Lucifer's realm, which enabled the Doyen to sense her daughters both on Earth and in Hell.

"Okay, so Winter's in Hell but why?"

"I do not know. Why would someone take Winter, of all of you, to Hell?"

It had been the same question racing back and forth in Izzy's brain. Why Winter, when you could scoop a real fallen angel?

"How do we save her?"

The Doyen moved to the large wooden bowl holding holy water. "I am at a loss."

"Can you venture into Lucifer's realm?"

The Doyen gave Izzy a penetrating look. "Not if I want to live. It would be a one-way ticket for me and I would not be able to get Winter out."

Izzy wanted to hit someone, preferably a demon with one of her blessed morning stars. "I will pray with my sisters and ask the same of you. In the meantime, we must perform tomorrow night and…"

"And you should recruit the humans to your cause," answered the Doyen.

"I am fearful you are correct. I do not like this choice but I can't see a clear path if we are to save the Heavens."

"I have something for you," said the Doyen, moving to a small wall cabinet. "This will provide strength for your lead singer."

Izzy gasped. "Is it what I think it is?"

"Yes. It's a feather from Lilith's wings. I have never had cause to utilize it. She said it would provide steadfast strength and aid in my time of need. This is our time of need. We must save Winter and we need aid for this heavenly fight. Now is the time to call on her aid."

Izzy didn't like that idea. The aid of Lilith would not be welcomed by the Mistress. Then again, the Mistress hadn't left them with one of her infamous angel feathers for help. If she had, Izzy would have called on her decades ago.

The Doyen took a red cloth from another drawer and wrapped the small black feather inside it. "Who is your lead singer?"

"Shea," said Izzy.

The Doyen handed the cloth to Izzy. "Do you feel she's up to this task?"

Another pressing question for the day. "I pray she is."

"More than prayer might be needed."

Izzy followed Doyen to the armory. "I do like when we see eye-to-eye."

"Take what you need. You and your sisters should be prepared in case demons show up at the recital."

That hadn't been on Izzy's radar. "What makes you think demons will come?"

"It's obvious."

Not to Izzy. "Explain."

"A demon has infiltrated your inner circle and knows your moves. This demon is dangerous because it wants something more than dead angels at the moment; telling in itself."

"Terrifyingly worrisome," muttered Izzy as she slid swords and more morning stars into the duffel bag the Doyen had pulled out of a hidden drawer.

"Trust no one," said the Doyen a few minutes later as Izzy prepared to venture back outside with her stash of weapons.

"I trust my sisters," said Izzy, with more bravado than clear knowledge.

"As Lilith trusted the Almighty once," said the Doyen, so quietly Izzy had to lean closer to hear her blasphemous words. "As I said, I will pray for us."

"Thank you," said Izzy, finally stepping back out to the sidewalk. It was no longer morning. Already mid-day, Izzy realized the last twelve hours felt like an eternity and there were a lot more hours in the day. When she returned home, they had to practice. She wondered about Gareth but had refrained from mentioning him to the Doyen. What had befallen him was a mystery she and Meredith would sort out. While she'd grown to trust the Doyen, she was her sisters' leader and ultimately the one responsible for their safety.

Izzy thought of the burden of her task as the duffel bag got heavier with each step closer to the brownstone, their home; a house which had been breached by a demon. She wanted answers. She could call on the Mistress but there was always a price for knowledge. Armed with her newfound angel wing feather, Izzy decided to hold off until after the recital. If they could recruit devoted humans to their cause they had hope. Wasn't hope what Heaven was all about? Or maybe that was love. Izzy felt out of her league but she'd experienced such before; when she'd first fallen to Earth shattered and alone.

She hefted the duffel bag up over her shoulder. She was no longer shattered and most certainly not alone. She had a family and a duty to uphold. By the heavenly scribes, I will not let my sisters down.

Two hours later, she and her fellow sisters were signing their hearts out. Shea's song was beautiful, heartfelt and soul-touching. They would need her divine touch tomorrow night.

"You did a lovely job," said Izzy to Shea.

"I fear I am not ready."

"Nonsense your voice is heavenly and now, more than ever, we need the miracle of your voice."

Shea gasped. "Meredith, what you say is sacrilegious. My voice is not a miracle."

"To us and humans it is. There is no shame in accepting the Almighty's gifts. He has blessed you with a heavenly voice and we, and all will benefit from your lyrical voice. Izzy, when should Shea sing the questing song?"

"It is a befitting finale piece," said Izzy.

"Great you want all the humans to run from the room," quipped Shea, causing both Izzy and Meredith to chuckle.

"They will not run from the room. Have no worry."

Izzy was about to say something else but Nayla entered. "Supper is ready."

"It smells divine," said Shea, quickly exiting the room.

"Meredith, what do you think of our Shea?" asked Izzy once Shea was gone.

"I think she is our sister and deserves our trust."

"Unwavering?" asked Izzy, which caused Meredith to turn and walk to the window.

"I will keep an eye on her. We can't forget what happened to her. It could have been any one of us."

But it wasn't. Izzy refrained from speaking such a statement. She was their leader and would defend all her fallen sisters with her own heavenly blood. Shea had taken up Izzy's quest for Cherub independence, and because of that had been expelled from the Heavens. On Earth she'd been brutally assaulted. Shea deserved her one hundred percent trust. It didn't mean it couldn't hurt to have Meredith keep a questing eye on her.

"You are correct, Meredith. It could have been any of us and Shea, more than any other, deserves our support. Thank you for keeping her utmost in your heart and prayers."

"As I do you too, Izzy," said Meredith, giving a brief smile as she too made her way to the dining room for nourishment.

"How fares Gareth?"

"I left Mike with him. After supper, I will check in on them. My prayer is he recovers quickly but as you know..."

"Being possessed by a demon for any length of time destroys the soul and mind," said Izzy.

"Gareth is a good man. He's lived a hard life on this Earth."

"Much like us," echoed Izzy, watching Meredith nod. "Then we must do all we can to heal our friend."

"We are of accord in this pursuit," said Meredith.

An accord built on hope, love and prayer, thought Izzy, not smiling with her realization as she took her seat as the table.

CHAPTER TWENTY-SIX

S hea was glad Ash had departed. She needed solace. His disclosure her twin was now the Queen of Hell felt like a blow to her soul. In the meantime, Ash was on a silent reconnaissance mission to find out why his sister had captured Winter. Any intel at this point would come in handy.

Shea lit a white candle and knelt to pray. Her mind tried to ease the thoughts zigging and zagging but after half an hour she knew it was a futile exercise. Standing, she turned to her bureau and quickly changed into her workout attire. Moving from her room into the hall, she was surprised to be confronted by Gareth.

"I know you," he said, looking unsteady on his feet and he leaned his weight against the wall.

Shea smiled shyly. "Of course, you know me, Gareth. You don't look well. Are you okay?"

"No. I know you but it was like my eyes saw you through another."

A shiver of alarm skirted through Shea. "Gareth, I don't understand what you are saying."

"Oh, Gareth, you are supposed to be in bed," said Meredith, saving Shea from having to continue her awkward conversation with the ex-soldier.

"I know her," muttered Gareth as he lent his body weight to Meredith.

Meredith gave Shea a perplexed look. "He is not well."

"Whatever has happened to him?" asked Shea.

"Aid me in getting him back to the bed."

Shea obliged and together they managed to ease Gareth back into the guest bedroom and under the covers.

"He is burning up," said Shea.

Meredith placed her hand on Gareth's brow. "Yes, he is. What did he say to you?"

"Nonsense, something about seeing me through eyes. It was perplexing."

Meredith went into the small bathroom adjacent to the room and returned with a bowl of water and cloth. She plunged the cloth into the water, and a heavenly scent filled the room.

"Is that holy water?" asked Shea.

"It is. Izzy and I fear Gareth has been possessed by a demon," said Meredith, sitting on the bed to administer the cooling balm to Gareth.

Shea did not gasp. True insight into what had happened to Meredith's friend blazed through her. Anger for what

Ash had done made her want to run from the room but she didn't dare.

"How can I be of assistance?" asked Shea.

Meredith smiled up at her. "A song from you would do wonders."

"I fear, Meredith, you place too much emphasis on the power of my voice, but I will oblige," said Shea.

Shea took a step closer to the bed and then closed her eyes. She searched through her repertoire of songs and finally found one she thought fitting for the ex-soldier. She let the heavenly ballad overtake her senses and found herself giving into the power of the verses. In the back of her mind, she heard Meredith gasp but didn't stop. Shea wasn't sure what possessed her but she leaned over Gareth and placed both hands over his heart. Heat the likes she hadn't known radiated out from her. When she felt the urge to get even closer, Ash's sharp angry voice ricocheted through her head.

Step away from the human, said Ash, his voice gravelly and angry, but crystal-clear in her mind.

Well, Shea was equally furious. He had knowingly possessed Gareth and to what end.

Shea if you don't take your hands off him, I will kill him.

Ash's statement did the trick. He meant what he said.

"Shea I have no idea what you did but he's looking measurably better. I told you there is power in your voice," said Meredith, not at all alarmed Shea had placed her hands on Gareth's body.

Shea gingerly stepped back. "I am glad to be of assistance. If you are okay, I will leave you. I thought to spend some time training."

"Yes, of course. Thank you once again for your help."

"It was my privilege," said Shea, finally exiting to make her way not to the training center but rather to her new destination, back to the Elie Wiesel Center for Judaic Studies.

Something was happening to her and she was determined to find answers. Thirty minutes later she strolled once again through the doors of the prestigious Jewish study center and no one gave her a second glance.

The interior of the place had been stamped in Shea's memory. She knocked on Daniel's door, pleased to find him inside.

"Come in," said Daniel.

Shea opened the door and immediately he stopped reading the book.

"Thank you, it's Shea. I hesitate to impose but..."

"You seek something from the library?"

"Yes."

"No problem, as soon as you return the book you borrowed," said Daniel, with more of an emphasis on the word 'borrowed' then Shea was comfortable with.

"I ask your forgiveness. You are correct, I borrowed the book and will most certainly return it."

Daniel stood up from his desk with a smile on his face. "No, it is I who should ask for forgiveness. I obviously didn't explain the system to you and I should never assume."

Shea laughed. "It seems these days everything has a system." And I fit in none. "Would it be possible to take a look through the library again and I pledge if I find a book, I will ask to borrow such."

Daniel came around to where Shea stood. "May I be of assistance in your search?"

"Well, to be truthful, I'm not sure what I'm looking for."

Daniel ushered Shea into the hall and then closed his office door. "You are seeking answers as to who you are and your faith."

"My faith is being tested and as to who I am, I fear that is also being subjected to a trial."

"Well then maybe together we can unite to find what you are in search of," said Daniel holding out his arm; a request for Shea to place her arm and in a way her faith, in his.

Together they made their way to the library. Daniel unlocked the door and the smell of leather and musty ancient books once again assaulted Shea's senses. Shea was sure her sister, Anya, would find the place holy. She did not.

Shea didn't know what she was looking for and prayed reading the titles would help.

"You read Hebrew?" asked Daniel, sounding surprised.

Shea smiled. She might be a fallen angel but she still had her skills. Speaking and reading all Earth languages was her skillset. It was something she shared with bookish Anya.

"Yes," replied Shea, hoping he'd drop it.

He turned and looked at her. Shea found his unseeing teal-colored eyes strangely salient.

"How many languages do you speak?"

"Many," she replied in his native tongue.

Daniel smiled. "You are a girl of mystery."

Shea gently touched his arm. "No, Daniel. I am a simple person."

He chuckled. "Of that, I truly believe you are wrong. Can you give me more of a hint to what you might be looking for?"

"A book describing the power of ancient songs."

"Oh, then we're in the wrong section. Follow me," said Daniel moving them deeper into the library. He used another set of keys to open a thick large door. Shea followed him to the back room. "How do you know where everything is?"

"I've memorized every book and its location in this library. It's why I am the only one allowed to return the books to their shelf and proper location. I don't want anyone messing up my order. These books are the oldest."

Shea looked at the ancient tomes. Many were leather-bound and they were voluminous with their scrolled knowledge.

"Thank you," said Shea.

"I will leave you to your quest. Drop by the office if you find the book you're looking for."

"I will," replied Shea.

Daniel deftly made his exit; a reminder for one born blind, he truly was in control of his environment.

Once he left, Shea closed her eyes and said a prayer to calm herself. I really should have asked for Anya's help. But Anya would have questions and as I don't have any answers which might please her, it's best that she remain in the dark. Reverently, Shea ran her fingertips along the old spines, hoping for a sign. Only when her fingers touched a smaller volume did she get a shock. Taking it as a sign, Shea pulled the tiny book free from its spot.

Written in the ancient Sumerian classical language, the book was very rare. The raised title on the spine was, "Endowment of Songs from Ereshkigal."

Ereshkigal was the goddess of Kur, the land of the dead or underworld in Sumerian mythology. By the feel of heat coming from holding the book, Shea felt certain this tome was what she sought.

Returning to Daniel's office, she was surprised to see him engrossed in a conversation with a student. As if he sensed her, Daniel looked in her direction.

"Do come in Shea," said Daniel, ushering her in.

Shea gingerly stepped into his office but kept close to the entranceway. She felt wary. She didn't know the young man and she didn't like the intensity of his scrutiny.

"Shea, this is Elon, the leader of the men's youth choir."

"Nice to meet you," said Shea, giving a slight bow with her head.

Elon smiled. "The pleasure is all mine. Daniel mentioned you were a student here but I confess to not seeing you before."

Shea had mastered the skillful art of omission and she most certainly had never said she was a student. Letting Daniel assume meant access to the wealth of knowledge in their library. Now, however, she was at a loss to explain herself or her actions.

"You know, I do believe I've seen you before. Yes, I know where. You sing in the Minstrel Singers band."

Shea smiled, saying thank you to the Almighty for the gift of song. "I do."

"You sing?" asked Daniel, clearly impressed.

"Yes, my fellow sisters and I formed a band."

"You're performing tomorrow night at the gala," stated Elon, giving her the traditional teenage male once-over.

"She is?" asked Daniel.

"I am," answered Shea, smiling and feeling more at ease with the situation. "Daniel, I really must go but I did want to let you know, I found a book I believe will be helpful. It's called Endowment of Songs from Ereshkigal. Would it be possible to borrow the script for a few days?"

"Oh yes," said Daniel, writing down the title on a piece of paper.

"Our group is also performing tomorrow night. We're the first set," said Elon, clearly looking to impress Shea.

"I'm not sure where we are in the line-up but I really must leave. Practice, as they say, makes perfect. Thank you once again, Daniel for your help. I hope to see you again soon."

"I will be at the gala, singing in the choir with Elon."

"Well then I'm sure our paths shall cross on tomorrow's blessed day," said Shea, quickly vacating the office before more questions could be volleyed her way.

Shea didn't waste time walking. She jogged home, anxious to read the ancient script and hopeful for any insight as to what was happening within her.

CHAPTER TWENTY-SEVEN

M eredith placed another cooling cloth on Gareth's head. "Thank you, Mike for sitting with him."

"What happened to him, Meredith?" asked Mike, casting a worried glance at Gareth.

It was hard for Meredith to understand that Mike and Gareth had a history as childhood friends when years later, they'd at first clashed. While an amicable friendship had developed over the years they were not close and Meredith wondered what had happened in their childhood to cause the rift. Meredith had known about the demons clawing at Gareth from day one when the ex-soldier had entered their lives. Looking back, she wondered if that was what drew her to him; the need to mother someone other than her sisters. Or, could it be, he reminded her in his own way of Zachary, the warrior who she and Izzy wooed to train them to kill demons. The same warrior who was a not-so-silent constant thought in her heart and soul. No good could come with her contemplation.

"We think he was possessed by a demon," said Meredith.

"I had wondered if it was possible," said Mike, arching his back.

Meredith suspected he'd been sitting in the hard-wooden chair for the past three hours. "You knew?'

"I suspected. The way he started to train the others in the center, it wasn't the moves I knew from Gareth."

"But you didn't say anything," said Meredith, careful not to sound accusatory.

"What could I say? Hey, Izzy, I think your friend, Gareth might be a demon."

"Yes, it would have helped."

"No, Meredith it wouldn't. Izzy is distracted, as are you these days and plus, I had no proof."

"I am not distracted," said Meredith.

"You are, but I get it. There is a lot of pressure on you and Izzy. There are days when I think about my newfound knowledge of angels and demons, I fear I shall lose my mind. I can't imagine the pressure facing you both."

Meredith breathed a sigh of relief. For a moment she feared his mentioning her distraction meant he knew about her history with Zachary. Sadly, she realized Mike was right. Zachary was distracting her from their goal. They had to form a workable army if they were going to save the Heavens.

"Thank you, Mike for your understanding. Did Izzy tell you about our plan for tomorrow night?"

"Yes. We went over it and I agree. We need to recruit more people and if there is a way to recruit humans to our cause without alarming the general public to mass hysteria," said Mike, with a chuckle, "then I'm glad. I will do what I can to help."

"You worry about this mass hysteria?"

"Meredith, humans like to think they are okay with the supernatural but the reality is we like our normal lives. It's comforting to think of Hell and Heaven as something in a fantasy land and something we don't have a say in. Realizing we might have to fight to keep our Heaven, and knowing angels and demons are real, could cause many humans to literally lose their minds. Our mental health is wired differently from you."

Meredith didn't know what to say. He spoke the truth.

"You fear for us and for all of mankind, Mike," said Meredith.

"Yes. I won't lie. The task set before you and now me, is daunting. If I think about it for too long, I do get overwhelmed. I also don't understand why more warrior angels won't come to your aid."

Meredith smiled. "Well, it is a simple truth. It's because we're the fallen."

"I know, but surely they understand more is at stake?"

"Trust me, they know but they hold firm in their belief nothing can penetrate the Heavenly Gates."

"Are they correct?"

"I pray daily they are correct but living on Earth has made me realize being prepared for the worst can create the best outcome for everyone," said Meredith.

Mike got up from the chair and stretched again. "I will take your advice and add it to my daily list of prayers."

"Since when did you start to pray?"

Mike turned to her and smiled. "Since the day I discovered you were all angels."

"Well, the Almighty will be blessed we had such a profound effect on you," said Meredith, wringing out the cloth in the basin filled with cool water to reapply to Gareth's forehead.

"Oh, I'm sure he'll have reason to rejoice. I'm going to head to the club for a while to deal with good old-fashioned accounts. They are boring and exactly what I need to curb my thoughts. I'll touch base later to see how he's doing. He's tough, Meredith, and I feel he'll get through this."

"We all pray for the Almighty's blessing," said Meredith. "Mike, would you mind asking Nayla to make a cup of the blessing tea for Gareth before you leave?"

"I won't even ask what that is but yes, I'll pop by the kitchen. If I'm lucky, something heavenly will be coming out of the oven," said Mike, finally exiting.

Meredith had a smile on her face as she watched Mike leave.

"I thought he'd never leave. We must talk," said Gareth, reaching out to grasp her wrist.

Meredith didn't like the ominous sound of his voice and the beads of perspiration on his forehead. He was taxing himself when he needed to rest and heal. "You must rest."

"No, we must talk. You're not going to like what I have to say."

Of that, Meredith knew in her heart, Gareth was correct.

Much of what Gareth told her didn't make sense. He was feverish and sounded delusional but Meredith knew he attempted to speak the truth.

"I was speaking with Shea. I felt this need to constantly be with her. Why?," said Gareth.

It was the question Meredith kept asking herself. Why Shea?

"I was in Hell, Meredith. I know it but..."

"But what?"

"This is going to sound strange."

"Stranger than what we've talked about?" asked Meredith, trying to lighten the mood. Gareth was burning up but determined to speak. She worried his font of information would overtask him.

Meredith got up from the chair to light another healing candle. Four were currently burning in the room and she hoped the light scent of lavender would calm him.

"Yes. Hell wasn't what I thought it would be like."

"What did you envision?"

"Oh, you know the usual, fire and brimstone but my sense of the space was one of palatial opulence."

This did surprise her.

"I'm not sure I was actually there, it's hard to explain, but it feels more like a memory."

"Does it feel the same as your thoughts about Shea?"

"No, those are much more intense. It's strange as I've never given her a second glance but I felt..."

"Felt what?"

"I felt we were connected."

"Connected in what way?" Meredith hating digging for answers.

"I can't explain it, but it felt like we were one. I...I...needed her," said Gareth, his eyes rolling back in his head with his final declaration.

Meredith knelt beside his bed. She pressed the cool cloth to his forehead and prayed he'd heal. She had more questions than answers and how did Shea fare in any of this?

A soft knock on the door drew her up sharply. "Come in."

Shea poked her head in. "How does he fare?"

Meredith looked at Shea. Yes, her outward appearance had changed but it wasn't her fault. The brutal attack leveled at her scarred her deeply.

"He is not well."

She stepped lightly into the room. "Would you like company praying?"

"Actually, would you mind singing to him, again?" Shea smiled. It was the type of smile which at one time had lit up the room.

"I would be honored," said Shea, moving closer to Gareth's bed.

Shea closed her eyes and Meredith watched her muster her courage. Shea started with an ancient hymn; the words soft but a tongue-filled ritual Meredith could never have mastered. Meredith kept applying the cloth but it was obvious within fifteen minutes the song was working. Gareth's breathing calmed and his forehead felt cooler.

Another gentle knock on the door had them both looking up.

"Yes?" asked Meredith.

Anya stood at the threshold of the door. "Meredith, Izzy wants to speak with you. She said it was urgent."

"Thank you, Anya. Tell Izzy I'm on my way," said Meredith, getting up off the floor.

Anya nodded and then departed.

"Shea, would you mind continuing to sing to him? Whatever you're doing, it's working for him."

"It would be my pleasure," said Shea.

Meredith placed one last cooling cloth on Gareth's head. She lingered by his side. Without conscious thought, Meredith reached out and touched Shea's hand, preparing herself to see a glimpse of Shea's future. Meredith's gift was to see the future when she touched people. She expected to glimpse something; in lieu of that she felt heat and saw only blackness.

"Are you well, Meredith?" asked Shea, clearly looking anxiously at her.

"Sorry. I worry about him."

"Our prayers are being answered. He will heal," said Shea, with such conviction, Meredith's heart warmed.

"You are correct, Shea. Our faith will mend him. Stay and sing to him. I must leave, or else Izzy will fly up here and disrupt the calm feeling we've created in his room."

"Izzy has a lot on her mind these days."

"As do we all," said Meredith, finally vacating the room. Gently, Meredith closed Gareth's door. She listened outside for a few minutes and was pleased to hear Shea start with a calm soothing hymn, one known to all Cherubs.

Walking downstairs, she found Izzy pacing in the living room.

"You have news?" asked Meredith.

"None you will like."

Meredith was the one this time claiming a seat. "Tell us what we need to do."

Izzy gave a mirthless laugh. "Oh, it's nothing too serious. We simply need to get into Hell to save Winter."

Sarcasm was Izzy's armor. Meredith understood how she wielded words like a blade. She knew keenly how this information, no, this impossible task, worried Izzy. Worse, she knew mounting a rescue mission into Hell would probably get them killed.

"We're going to rescue her?" asked Meredith.

Izzy knelt next to Meredith. "We must. She followed our path. We owe her this."

"What about the Doyen?"

"She can't help."

Can't or won't? "Izzy, we have to sing tonight. For the greater good we must recruit more humans to our heavenly army."

"Meredith, we can't simply leave her there."

"You must," said Zachary, stepping into their space.

Immediately Izzy stood. "We don't take orders from you."

Zachary ignored Izzy. "Meredith is correct. We must stay on course. Tonight, is your chance to recruit humans and ..."

Izzy marched over to Zachary. "You didn't want us to recruit humans and now you've changed your mind. Why?"

"I'm adapting to Earth. We need to be prepared and I feel you also have changed your mind."

"Who is this "we" you are referring to?" asked Izzy, looking ready for a fight.

Meredith stood up and moved between the two. "Zachary is correct. We've worked too hard to halt our plans. You know we won't get another invite to sing and we must seize the opportunity."

"But what about Winter?" There was an ache in Izzy's voice Meredith understood. When they were banished to Earth, Izzy had been alone. The rest of them had each other but she'd lived years in solitude in this guise of a human teenager and life and faith had not been easy for her.

"After the recital we will plan a way to save her," said Meredith.

"I hope we're not too late," said Izzy, departing.

Only when Izzy was truly gone did Zachary step closer to Meredith. "We might not be able to save her."

"But we're going to try."

"Your strategy doesn't make sense. Why risk all for one?"

Meredith gave him a penetrating look. "Because it is who we are and what we stand for. We are united in our cause and one is not more than the sum of us all."

Zachary gave her a strange look. "I have never understood your faith in this but I will help."

"You sure you don't want to stay on the sidelines like you're used to?" snapped Meredith. She had enough for the day. Worry about Gareth had taxed her and thinking something might be wrong with Shea left her feeling off.

"You were never like this in the Heavens," said Zachary.

Meredith moved closer. "I was but you didn't see or hear me. I was simply a Cherub. I had a predestined role to serve. I'm glad all has changed. This is the real me,

Zachary. I have a voice and my own free will. We don't need your help."

Zachary smiled. "Meredith, you are correct but my eyes are open now and I quite like what I see and hear. I will help. You're not getting rid of me so easily."

Why did his look and statement make her nervous?

"I need to rest. It's been a taxing day," said Meredith, moving around Zachary to escape. She wanted to run and as if he knew it, she heard the mighty warrior chuckle.

"Our time will come," he said.

Was there a note of hope in his voice or was it simply Meredith's wishful thinking? Rest, exactly what she needed if she was going to be in any shape for the recital. Thinking of what they were trying to accomplish was both blissful and overwhelming. Then again, as fallen angels, they had been accomplishing the impossible since arriving on Earth well over a decade ago.

Never underestimate the fallen, thought Meredith as a smile tugged at her lips.

CHAPTER TWENTY-EIGHT

"**I** know you," said Gareth.

Shea wasn't sure at first she'd heard him correctly. She leaned closer to the ex-soldier on the bed.

"What?"

"I know you," he rasped.

"I'm one of Meredith's sisters. You are unwell. I am helping to heal you."

Gareth reached out to touch her arm. "No. I have this connection to you and I don't know why. I...I'm not myself."

Shea tucked his arm back under the blanket. She had to compose herself. Her heart was beating erratically. Shea prayed for guidance or a sign as to how best proceed.

Something is bothering you. Are you safe? asked Ash, his voice a calm balm to her racing heart and mind.

I am fine but we have a situation.

What do you mean a situation?

You shouldn't have possessed Gareth. I'm here with him now and he's saying he knows me.

Are you alone with him, Shea?

There was an edge to Ash's voice, which Shea sadly liked. It felt possessive but she would not ever admit this to the demon who had changed her life irreversibly. Yes. I had been singing a healing chant to him with Meredith.

I need you to sing a different type of chant to him.

Shea cast her eyes to the door. What do you have in mind?

A chant to make him forget and give him a semblance of peace.

Ash, my aim is to heal him.

This, my b'iã, will heal him. He needs to forget about you.

Shea pondered his statement and her heart knew Ash spoke the truth. Tell me the name of the chant.

The words he spoke sang to Shea and instantly she knew the song.

"Why do I feel this need to be with you?" asked Gareth, reminding Shea she had a task to accomplish fast.

"I'm going to sing a special healing song to you Gareth, which will help heal you."

Gareth sighed as he leaned back into his pillow. Shea took a moment to let the ancient biblical knowledge of the song sink into her heart. Then she laid a hand over Gareth's heart and began. She closed her eyes and the room and time dissolved. Shea lost herself in the ancient words, feeling a fire she had never known as it encompassed her. She wasn't sure how long she sang but at the last verse, she added a few prayerful words. Instant cold surged through her hands. The connection to the song ended as sharp as a sword's blade. Exhausted, Shea grabbed the wooden chair.

Not a minute too soon, thought Shea, as Meredith barged into the room.

"Shea, my blessed sister you look exhausted. Have you been singing this entire time?" asked Meredith, instantly placing a hand on Gareth's forehead. "I believe his fever has broken. Thank you, Shea."

Shea swallowed and slowly released her hand from the chair. "I am honored to have been able to help. You are correct, Meredith. I am tired."

"Go and rest. I will have Nayla bring supper to your room."

Shea nodded. The need to escape felt overwhelming. Slowly she exited the room only to almost crawl up the flight of stairs back to the solitude of her room. The minute she closed her door and locked it, yes she'd gotten into the habit to ensure no one walked in unannounced, Ash scooped her up off the floor.

"You have overtaxed yourself and I will not have that," he said, laying her, with his usual reverence, on her bed.

When he went to remove himself, Shea was the one who pulled him down into her bed. "Stay," said Shea, feeling her lids almost close.

He flashed one of his devilish grins at her and then did as instructed.

"Your wish, my b'iã, I willingly concede to."

Shea wanted to say something witty but her exhaustion was truly overwhelming. The heat of his body and arms as he pulled her closer lulled her into the abyss of sleep and her last thought was she hoped the song helped the ex-soldier because what Ash did to him was unthinkable. Shea vowed when she reclaimed her energy she'd let Ash know exactly how she felt; anger, not the desire scorching her body and heart she said to herself, knowing it was a lie.

CHAPTER TWENTY-NINE

T he power shake-up in Hell was not to Ash's liking. Having a Queen of Hell assert her position, a seat left vacant since Lilith's departure, had enabled Ash to scheme his way forward. Having his father distracted was always best. The thought he might be still distracted with his new Queen was not lost on Ash. However, he didn't trust this new Queen, whose faith seemed vengeance filled against the angels. She yearned to tear the Gates of Heaven open and let her fellow twin angels, discarded to die in The Precipice, wreak havoc. Thankfully, most of those angels they'd rescued were still recovering. Each of them had been given the choice to live, which meant ingesting demon blood, and not one had said no. Living was for the strong.

A knock at Shea's door had him bolting out of bed.

Shea stirred. She quickly gave him a shushing look and then responded to the knock. "Yes."

"I brought you supper and we're to meet in about an hour in the lobby before we go to the recital," said Nayla.

"Thank you, Nayla. You may leave it by the door. I fell asleep and will dress and retrieve my food. Thank you so much for your kindness."

"As always, it is my pleasure to serve," said Nayla. "Good luck tonight with your blessed voice."

Ash gave Shea a perplexed look as they both heard the platter being placed on the floor.

"I wish I could hear you sing tonight. I confess to being envious of the humans tonight who get to see and hear your heavenly voice."

Shea moved closer to him. "You like my heavenly voice?"

Ash scooped her body closer to his, so she could straddle him. "Your voice will always please me but the power of your voice could bring demons to their knees."

Shea leaned into him, letting her lips gently graze his. "I think you place too much power, like my sisters, in my ability."

Ash's hand snaked through her long hair, pulling her closer. "You like to tease and this pleases me."

"And you like to be in command."

"Correct," said Ash, finally claiming Shea's lips in a heated kiss. He envisioned slinking into bed with her but she playfully escaped his clutches.

"I have to eat and get ready for the recital."

"Are you telling me I must leave?"

"Yes, and you know it."

"Why is it you sound like the one in command?" teased Ash. He enjoyed watching Shea move. She was naturally graceful. She balanced the food tray with ease and sat cross-legged on the bed to eat.

"You're staring," said Shea, holding a hot bun with melting butter in her hand.

"At you always."

"Stop it. It's unnerving."

Ash took a bite of her hot bun and enjoyed watching her eyes widen at his playfulness. "They will be staring at you tonight. Can you handle it, Shea?"

That had her gulping and a blush stole over her cheeks making her look younger and deliciously cute. "I will do my duty."

Ash tisked. "A lie and you boldly know it. You enjoy the limelight, as they say and it's nothing to be ashamed of. I am proud of your strong will."

"You are?"

"Yes, of course. Our path is not an easy one."

"I'm not sure I recall agreeing to your path. Remind me again what you speak of?"

Me ruling Hell and you at my side as my Queen. Ash wisely kept silent. "A discussion for another time. I must go to my realm and ensure my sister has not harmed Winter."

"Speaking of Winter, can you rescue her for us?"

"I wish I could, but my sister would know and then my father..."

"Would know...I get it. What do you suggest we do to help Winter?"

Ash moved closer to the fire. "Kali has assured me Winter will not be harmed."

"And do you believe her?"

"She can't lie to me. A telling of a lie I would scent from her. The better and bigger question is why did she take Winter?"

"Maybe they are connected?"

"What?" asked Ash, turning his head to watch Shea finish with her meal.

"Gareth said he felt connected to me when you possessed him and don't forget I am mad at you and have not forgiven you for his ill treatment. Winter has your sister's blood, so maybe they are connected."

Ash hadn't thought about the connection. "You can't still be mad at me for what I did to Gareth. My reasons were in your best interests. I did what had to be done. I won't apologize for my actions."

"Ash, you can't go around possessing people."

"Shea, I did it for you. I had to be close to you. I had to make sure you were safe."

"You hurt Gareth."

"That ex-soldier is bloody well tough. More like he hurt me. What a hassle to possess him," said Ash, enjoying the feel of heat from the fireplace. .

"My poor baby, was he screaming in your head to release him?" teased Shea.

"Yes, my b'iã, he was and it was annoying. If I killed him, you'd be mad so I didn't. Pleased?"

Shea gave him a crafty smile. "Of course, I'd be mad if you killed him. He's an innocent."

Ash choked on a laugh. "Trust me he's not. I've been in his head and innocent that man is not."

"Well, he is an ex-soldier. Anyway, you are distracting me. I'm having a shower and preparing myself for the recital tonight."

"I shall leave you and check in on my sister and her nefarious plans."

Shea walked over to where he stood by the fire and gave him a kiss. "Be safe," she said, repeating his earlier warning to her.

"And you. I will return tonight."

Shea smiled. "I shall look forward to your visit."

Ash gave her a last lingering kiss and watched her walk into her private bathroom. He longed to spend more time with her but he also needed to watch closely what was happening at home, in Hell. Casting his mind to his realm, Ash plunged into the fire, sighing in extasy as heat consumed him. Returning to the safety of his room he waited a few minutes and then made his way to where his sister resided in the north corridor. The gate to the north corridor was locked and four guards were marshaled behind it.

"It's Ash you idiots, her brother, let me in."

They didn't answer. Knowing Kali, she probably had their tongues removed. Well, there were other ways to invade his sister's domain. Turning to smoke, Ash scaled the walls unseen and seeped into Kali's room. The sight in her private bedroom was not one he expected. Kali and Winter were in bed asleep and his sister had a possessive arm around her captive. Ash was beginning to wonder if Winter was truly being held against her will. By the sensual pose of the two, he highly doubted it.

Forming into his solid body, Ash gave a cough.

"Did you honestly think I didn't know it was you in my bedroom?" asked Kali.

Ash smiled. "Did you tire her out with your questioning?"

Kali nudged a pillow up behind her head and a tug of a smile claimed his sister's lips. When they were young it had been an everyday occurrence but once they came of age, Lucifer made sure to quickly erase her grin.

"What do you want, brother dear?"

"More like what do you want? Why did you steal Winter?"

Kali looked over at the still sleeping Winter. "I did not steal her. She asked for my help."

This Ash had not expected. "Then why the ruse of smoke?"

"Unlike you, Ash, I couldn't simply walk into the angel's house."

"I don't walk in," said Ash.

"Please, the fact you're in love with an angel is comical. Does our father know of your recent exploits?"

"Leave well enough alone."

Kali ran a gentle hand along Winter's back, which was covered with a plush red blanket. Red was Kali's signature color. She said it reminded her of blood, which was another favorite of his sister.

"How about a truce? I will leave you to your Winter and you will stay out of my business."

Kali pursed her lips. "And what is this business you feel I should stay out of?"

"None of your business. But I will tell you this, the angels will not rest until Winter is once again with them."

"I did not steal her. She asked for my help and what do you know, we clicked."

Ash rolled his eyes. "I can see you clicked but she has to go back."

"What if she doesn't want to?"

"I'm not going to argue with you but these angels are resourceful and she's sort of one of them."

His sister laughed. "She's so far from an angel it's hilarious."

"What?"

Kali slid out of the bed and motioned for Ash to follow her to her sitting room. "Ash, did you know earth-born angels are made by Lilith?"

"No, impossible," said Ash. What game was Lilith up to? Kali had always been obsessed with anything related to Lilith, who was her mother. Thankfully, not the case for Ash.

"It's true. Earth-born angels are more like us, demons," said Kali with a smile.

"Then why do they fight us?"

"To get their wings," said Kali.

Ash thought there was more to it than Kali knew. She always plunged headfirst into things concerning her mother because of her abandonment issues. Ash refrained from mentioning such. The last time they had a discussion centered around Lilith, Ash had watched his father kill Kali and then had been thrown into a pit for years. Knowing it was now all a charade left him with mixed feelings. Kali, alive, was Lucifer's pawn and now it seems Lilith's as well.

"Do you think our father knows of this?"

Kali gave a scornful laugh. "Highly doubtful."

"But why would Lilith help humans?"

Kali poked her head into the other room to ensure her sleeping companion still slumbered. "I don't know but I plan to find out. Winter called to me and I came to her."

"Did you think she might be using you?"

Kali blinked and gave him a crafty smile. "Of course, it's the charm."

"Keeping her here in Lucifer's realm is not safe. He has spies everywhere."

"Not in my space. You can be sure."

"I wouldn't be so cocky. Take her back."

"What if she doesn't want to leave? I'm sort of addictive," said Kali, grinning.

Ash couldn't suppress his own grin. More like the angel hybrid demon human is the addictive one. "If you have any feelings for her it's best to remove her from this realm. I will leave this decision in your capable hands. I'm being summoned."

"Father is summoning you?"

Ash nodded, as his body turned to smoke, not of his own volition. When his father's temper was at its height, he forced those he wanted to see to come to him whether they wanted to or not.

"Why is he not calling me?" screamed Kali.

Ash wasn't grinning when he rematerialized at the feet of his father, who sat perched on his throne of skulls. Next to him, in a similar chair, sat the new Queen of Hell. He was about to pray Kali listened to his reasoning but taking a quick look at his father's face, he dug his knees into the pebbled floor and sought the pain to ground him. Praying in his father realm for all Ash knew might be something Lucifer could sense. Getting killed was not on his agenda.

Dismantling Shea's sister from her newfound perch and toppling his father off his self-made godly throne, most certainly, was utmost in Ash's mind.

"You called, father?"

"It seems, son, you have been remiss in introducing me to your latest treasure."

Ash swallowed but didn't dare cast a glance at the Queen. So much for loyalty. Ash tried hard to think how not to lie to his father while keeping Shea safe.

"Yes, Ash do tell your father all about her," said Isis, with a cunning look of pleasure on her face.

It would make Shea mad, him killing her sister, but the task had moved to the top of Ash's priorities.

CHAPTER THIRTY

They were assembled inside the Luxury Parkview Suite of The Ritz-Carleton. Someone had brought cocktails for them. Not one sister touched the colorful concoctions. Alcohol did not mix well with angel DNA.

Izzy highly suspected, as they had walked through the entrance on Avery Street into the foyer of the posh hotel, their dress attire wasn't appreciated.

Most wore their usual outfit; a short pleated black and white skirt, high-top red sneakers with black laces and white blouses tied into halter tops. The only one who wore something different was Shea. She was dressed in black leather pants with boots climbing past her knees and a black halter top. Izzy thought she looked stunning. The fact their teenage guise wasn't one they could discard often made Izzy angry, especially when she had to deal with humans who thought teenagers, like her, couldn't manage a band.

It took fifteen minutes before the manager agreed to let them into the suite. It had been in their contract and Izzy would not relent. They needed time, alone, before singing to pray and tonight would not be an exception.

Izzy looked over at Anya who had once again cut her hair into her usual pixie-cropped style she liked to wear on stage. Tonight, she'd dyed the ends of her hair purple.

"Are you ready?" asked Izzy to Shea.

Shea nodded but her eyes kept darting to the expanse of windows. Boston at night was stunning. "It's beautiful isn't it?"

"Yes," answered Izzy. "You sure about singing the last song?"

Shea turned to give her full attention to Izzy. "I won't let you down."

Izzy wanted to reach out and touch Shea but knew better. The pain of knowledge she'd glean from Shea would crush her and tonight she needed to be one hundred percent. The show must go on, thought Izzy.

"I know you won't. We all have faith in you."

A knock at their door was the signal they had fifteen minutes until show time. Meredith urged them into a circle and they all bowed their head in prayer.

"Tonight, we must recruit humans to our cause. By the blessed power of prayer, we pray for his Almighty's grace in this divine task the Mistress has entrusted this to us. Together, we are united and steadfast in His grace and we ask his Almighty's blessing," said Izzy, wondering if any of her fallen sisters heard his divine voice, because she didn't.

As they lined up, Izzy approached Shea again. "This is for you," she said, opening the red cloth to reveal Lilith's feather.

"What is it?"

"The Doyen said it was given to her by their creator, Lilith."

"Lilith?" gasped Shea, backing up from the gift.

Izzy well understood her reaction. Quickly Izzy explained in as brief points as she could how Lilith had created the Earth-bound angels.

"Are you sure I should be the one to hold this?" asked Shea, clearly uncomfortable with the notion.

"Yes. You are singing the most important song of the night. This will give you strength," said Izzy urging Shea to take the small black feather.

With reverence and a good touch of fear, Shea took the feather. Izzy smiled when she tucked it into her hair.

"Thank you, Shea," said Izzy.

Shea remained silent and it was Meredith who urged Izzy to the front. Now was the time to place their plan into action. They had this one opportunity and could not mess it up.

Izzy marched her sisters to the elevator, praying for renewed strength and guidance. They hadn't sung as a band to a crowd in a long time. While she didn't question their skill, tonight what she was asking of her sisters was different. They had to sing like the Cherub angels they were if they hoped to save their home; a place they'd been exiled from for eternity. There was irony in their quest, but more than anything Izzy felt sadness for her fellow sisters' predicament. They had followed her for independence and because of her actions they were the fallen.

"Your thoughts betray you, Izzy. You worry for us," said Meredith.

Izzy reached out and hugged Meredith. "What would I do without you?"

"Never stay out of trouble, or maybe get into trouble with Nathanael," said Meredith with a chuckle.

"He's planning to attend tonight."

"By the blessed light, of course he is. He wouldn't miss seeing you sing on stage. Do you think he got an invite?"

"Invite or no, he'll be here. He's worried demons will attend."

"Are you worried?"

Izzy leaned into her. "I am hopeful. Killing demons would actually make this night."

"It would, but mass hysteria of humans must be avoided."

"Now you are sounding like Zachary."

"Don't be mean," teased Meredith.

The elevator dinged. They were at the floor leading to the ballroom. Izzy threw a wink at Meredith and then led her fellow sisters down the psychedelic carpeted hallway to the back-door entrance to the ballroom.

"Nice to see you again," said a young man to Shea.

Shea gave a shy smile. "Sorry I missed the opportunity to hear you sing, Daniel."

Izzy was about to question Shea when the young man whipped out a cane. He was blind. This surprised Izzy.

"I hope you will visit us again soon."

"I must to return the book," said Shea.

"Shea, we must get into formation," said Izzy, urging her sister to the stage.

"Sorry. I will see you soon, Daniel," said Shea, moving away to take her place on the stage.

"Not before I see you first," said the young man with a beaming smile.

The pun was not lost on Izzy. As to how Shea knew the stranger, Izzy would question later. Izzy took her place, center stage, pleased to see her fellow sisters all in position. The lights went dark. The throng of voices fell silent. This was the moment, sweet anticipation that Izzy loved.

She started with a soft hum, letting the power of the song soar through her heavenly being. Only when her fellow sisters joined her did the lights come back onto the stage to illuminate them. The place was packed with people. The men wore tuxedos or black suits and the women wore silky ballgowns of varying shades. There at the back stood her Nathanael, her warrior, his eyes hooked onto her as she sang with all her might. He was a reminder, he believed in her cause for independence, where she would lead an army to keep the Heavens safe, and for that, Izzy was falling more in love with the warrior by the day. Who would have thought he'd sacrifice so much for a Cherub who still refused to truly bind with him to become his b'iã. Certainly not Izzy, recalling the first time she'd met the warrior who'd had a not-so-close encounter the minute he'd landed on Earth with a demon. She wondered again if the Mistress had played a role in her saving him on that eventful night. If so, she wasn't sure if she was supposed to be angry or thankful for the Mistress role.

CHAPTER THIRTY-ONE

They were into their second set when the doors to the ballroom flew open. Shea watched her sister saunter into the room. She was dressed similar to Shea, black leather pants and a tight bodice which outlined her beautiful adult figure. But she had long white hair which was braided. In her right hand was a sword. The sight of the weapon alarmed Shea. It took her a moment to realize her twin wasn't alone. Walking like a well-orchestrated army behind her were about a dozen demons.

Izzy faltered in her song. Isis inched closer to the stage. Shea wasn't sure what possessed her but she stepped forward. The feather, tucked behind her ear, started to burn.

Izzy ran to the side of the stage. Shea highly suspected she was getting weapons. Shea did not want to fight her sister. Not sure she was doing the right thing, she started to sing. The song she'd discovered in the ancient book rolled off her tongue and the power of the words had the demons falling to their knees. Isis covered her ears. Shea did not falter. She kept singing, absorbing the power from the ancient hymn.

The humans finally clued into the fact it was not part of the act. Screams erupted to fill the chaos of the room, as people started to run for the exits. Still Shea stood tall and kept singing. Izzy tucked a sword into her hand, the cool steel momentarily making her lose the cadence of the song and a second later a demon jumped up on to the stage. Before Shea could think, Meredith staked the demon through the heart, making it dissolve into smoke.

"Keep singing," said Meredith, jumping from the stage to join the melee.

The minute Shea had stopped the song, the demons regrouped, getting up off their knees to form a tight circle around Isis, guarding her like the sovereign she had become.

Shea was about to open her mouth to sing when Isis stepped through her guards and pointed a hand at her. Even over the throng of hysterical screams, Shea heard her sister's words. Spoken in the demon language, one Shea didn't know she understand until that moment, her eyes widened. Her sister was stealing her voice.

Not sure what possessed her, Shea took Lilith's feather and placed it across her throat. Isis stopped speaking.

"That does not belong to you," said Isis, attempting to move forward.

"Sing," screamed Izzy, hurling a morning star, obviously dipped in holy water, at a demon. The demon died in a puff of sulfur.

Shea closed her eyes, praying her sisters would ensure her safety and sang. This time it was different. She didn't waste time with the first verse, she went to the last; the words forced the demons to heel and Isis screamed in annoyance.

Kneeling demons made them easy to kill and her sisters didn't waste time. It took minutes and in was then Shea realized something. She had power.

Isis jumped up to the stage, next to Shea.

"Enjoy the taste of power, sister of my blood," said Isis, a crafty smile lighting her face.

Shea did, but knew enough to refrain from acknowledging the euphoric high coursing through her veins.

"Why are you here?"

"Heard you were having a little sing-song so had to see for myself," said Isis, casting a look out at the crowd of frantic humans. "I must say the taste of human fear is truly addictive. And you have surprised me."

"Me?"

Her twin moved closer and the weight of the sword in Shea's resting palm felt insurmountably heavy.

"You have the gift of song, or is it a curse? I'm still learning all this demon, angel thing and honestly it's confusing."

Shea almost smiled. "What do you want?"

"To see you all in action and..." said Isis, throwing out her elegant arm to indicate the crowd, "this is interesting."

"Interesting?"

"I heard you're looking to recruit an army. I plan to stop you," said Isis, walking even closer.

Only an arm's length separated them. Shea had thought saving her sister would make her feel whole, would make her yearn to hug her twin and finally feel connected to being all it meant to be a Cherub, but she had been wrong. The dream did not equate to the reality. The pulse of the sword in her palm felt like a counter-measure.

"Do you plan to use your sword on me?" asked Isis, tisking and tossing a wink at her. "I think not. It's time I left. Good to see you sister and it pleases me to know we're not so dissimilar."

"You shouldn't have come," said Shea, noticing Izzy moving through the crowd toward the stage.

"I'm glad I came. Oh, is she your leader? Ash told me all about her. I think I'd like her."

"You must go," said Shea, surprising herself by moving her sword up.

Isis cocked her head to the side. "Have you told them yet about me? Ah, I think not. Then again they don't know about Ash either. Lots of secrets in your angel house you now call home."

"Please go," said Shea, her eyes darting around the room. Meredith was falling into stride behind Izzy and they were both heading to the stage. The last thing Shea wanted was for them to kill her sister.

"Should we make it seem like we're fighting? Give them a show, sis?"

"Just go," said Shea.

"On one condition," said Isis.

"What?"

"I've come to you twice, now it's your turn. Promise you'll visit me in Hell."

"What? I can't go there."

"Oh yes you can, and you know it. You have demon blood in those veins like me. Visit me."

"For all I know you'd trap me there."

"I promise I won't. I want to talk to you. I want to get to know you."

The lure undid Shea. "Fine. I'll visit. Now you must go."

"You're going to have hit me with that thing," said Isis, her eyes flashing to the sword in Shea's hand.

Shea knew she was correct. Both Izzy and Meredith were almost to the stage. "Okay, when I swing..."

Shea was about to explain more when Nathanael raced from the side exit. In the next instant, Isis pushed Shea away while grabbing her sword at the same time. Within seconds Nathanael and Isis were in a deadly battle.

"Get off the stage!" shouted Izzy, getting ready to jump onto the stage to help Nathanael eliminate her twin.

Shea didn't know what to do. Isis was tiring and her hand was burned as the entire sword had been dipped in holy water. If she had been fully demon she'd have burst into flames by now. When she slipped on a cord running across the stage, everything went slow motion for Shea. She saw Nathanael heave his sword up and knew he was within seconds of arching it for a killing blow for her twin. Without thinking and going on instinct, Shea felt her wings unfurl as she threw her body between his blade and her twin. The impact of the blade on her wings was brutal but angel wings were super strong, allowing her body to absorb the blow so her sister lived.

Gasps tore through the ballroom. Shea had done the unthinkable. She'd exposed them all to humans. Lifting her head, she caught Meredith and Izzy's horrified expression. Then it dawned on Shea why. Her once white wings were now black, a cast to the demon she feared she was becoming.

"I most certainly didn't expect your help. Thanks so much for saving me, sister. See you soon," said Isis and then in a puff she disappeared.

Shea barely took a breath. Every eye in the room zeroed in on her. She quickly made her wings invisible.

"Sing the song," said Izzy. "The last song. We need to recruit them."

Surprised her fellow sister was still speaking to her, Shea was shocked. Straightening, she closed her eyes and let the pull of the song burn through her. It was a song of grace while asking for one to have strength and faith.

When it was finished, Shea was shaking. Izzy walked over to her and gave her a hug, surprising Shea. Then in a move shocking Shea to the core, Izzy moved to the center of the stage and spoke.

"For those of you with faith, we are the fallen angels tasked to save the Heavens. As you saw tonight demons are on Earth and yes, angels too, and we've come tonight to ask for your help. A demon army is amassing and the heavenly realm is in danger. Step forward if your belief is steadfast, true and if you are willing to join our fight."

"It was part of the act," said a young man.

Izzy looked at Shea. "An act. Sisters I think they need a bit more proof. Show your heavenly wings and come to me."

"What?" squeaked Shea as she watched all her fallen sisters proudly display their beautiful ivory-colored wings.

"Including you, Shea," said Izzy.

"But my...

"It's okay. Do as I have asked," said Izzy.

Shea bowed her head and then did as instructed. She felt Meredith come up to her side to grasp her hand. Only once all her sisters had flown to the stage and they were all linked by hand did it truly dawn on the humans the truth of Izzy's words.

"I need fighters. Who will join us?"

Shea couldn't help but smile when Daniel's voice was the first she heard.

"I will," said Daniel, stepping forward.

Within seconds most of the young males in the room had stepped forward but what astonished Shea was the fact every single young woman in the room too had stepped forward.

"We carry our faith and if the Almighty needs our help we will willingly join his army," said a young woman, her voice strong with purpose even if she looked ridiculous wearing a puffy yellow prom-looking dress which made her bottom look like a muffin.

Izzy smiled. "Thank you. Meredith here is my second-in-command. She will provide you all with details on where and when we train. For tonight, go home and enjoy your time with your family. Now before we leave I will lead us in one final song."

Izzy sang a song of divine prayer and heavenly grace but it was also one to make them all forget what had happened. They would remember the details Meredith gave them for a proper meeting tomorrow but Izzy had to control the situation. Humans truly understanding angels and demons existed didn't make a good mix. When the song was finished, Izzy was the one to lead Shea off the stage.

"When we get back home we need to have a talk," said Izzy.

Shea's legs felt like lead as she followed her fellow sisters down the hall to finally escape the hotel. "I know."

"Are you okay?" asked Anya, moving to her side the minute Izzy continued with her normal march-like walk.

"Not really," said Shea, feeling ashamed.

"You should have told us. What happened to you isn't your fault."

Shea wasn't so sure.

"Do you know who that woman was who was leading the demons?"

Shea felt her heart race. "Yes."

Anya gave her a quick glance. "I thought as much. Is this why you've been sneaking out to go to the library?"

"What? You knew about the library?"

Anya gently took her hand. "We all have secrets, Shea. None of us are saints. We're the fallen for a reason. The first time I saw you in the library, I couldn't believe it. I wanted to ask you but realized you were searching for something like me."

"What were you looking for?"

"Answers," said Anya and on that cryptic word she gave Shea's hand a squeeze.

Shea mulled Anya's conversation over in her head. She was surprised her bookish sister had divulged so much. Maybe she wasn't so alone with her secrets.

Meredith opened the brownstone and they all, in their subdued way, scuttled in.

"I'm going to change and then will talk with you and Izzy in the prayer room," said Shea.

Meredith gave her arm a slight squeeze but she wore a tight smile. "I will bring us some refreshments."

"Thank you," said Shea, walking up the stairs into her room.

She changed quickly into a more relaxed attire; black leggings and a light blue sweater. She should have been hot after all which had transpired but cold goosebumps clamored on her skin. When Shea walked into the prayer room, she wasn't surprised to see both Meredith and Izzy had also changed.

"I'm so sorry," said Shea, accepting the hot chocolate from Meredith.

"It is we who should be apologizing. We haven't been there for you," said Izzy.

"What happened to you wasn't your choice," said Meredith.

"Off course it wasn't her fault," said Izzy.

Shea felt tears gather. Her sisters were defending her but they didn't know the whole truth and she feared disfavor if she mentioned Ash.

"I need to tell you something," said Shea.

Do not tell them. Ash's voice boomed loud in her head. She understood his concern but keeping this secret, along with her twin's existence felt wrong.

Shea took a deep breath. "I have a twin."

All the idle chatter ceased.

"It's why I joined your cause. I wanted to save her."

You really shouldn't tell them this, said Ash.

Shea could have sworn she heard him sigh.

"And did you?" asked Meredith, pulling her down to sit on the sofa which lined the wall.

Shea didn't know what to say. She hadn't really been the one to save her sister, but Ash had. Would her sisters understand?

No, they would not, said Ash, a harsh reminder he heard her inner battle.

Was her sister truly saved?

"You are both not going to like what I have to say."

Izzy reached out and gave her hand a squeeze. "The truth is the hardest, but know this, Shea, you are our sister...a fallen angel and we will always have your back."

Meredith nodded.

I beg of thee, do not, said Ash.

Shea closed her eyes and prayed for the courage she needed as she pointedly ignored her lover's pleas. She wasn't sure how long she spoke but she told them everything from the beginning time in the Heavens. She told them how she joined their plight in the Heavens for selfish reasons to find a way to save her twin; a twin no one acknowledged but deep within Shea's heart and soul she knew the truth– she had a twin sister and her destiny was to save her. When it came to the night of her so-called assault, it was a harder truth to unearth. She had been on her way to sing in a choir, she'd been sneaking out of the house nightly to find a way to release her anguish and find some solace and singing in a choir did the trick. When the demons came at her in the alley she'd been stunned and further surprised when her savior turned out to be a demon; and not just any demon, rather Lucifer's son. Shea told her sisters how she'd spent the night talking to Ash, Lucifer's son, and how he gave her a choice; he could return her unharmed or if he took her innocence he'd claim a part of her angel power and it would enable him to be fully independent of his father's realm and he'd help her in her personal quest. They knew the rest and wisely refrained from speaking the burning question hanging unsaid in the room; why had she acquiesced. Shea then launched into her quest for Ash to find her sister, and how he saved her twin, but there was a problem. Her twin sister wanted nothing to do with the heavenly realm of her origins and since Lucifer helped to heal her, she'd since claimed the title of Queen of Hell.

"Let me make sure I understand everything. Lucifer's son made a deal with you and you agreed so you could save your sister and now your twin has appointed herself the Queen of Hell," said Izzy.

"Yes, correct," said Shea.

"Why did you not talk to us sooner?" asked Meredith.

"Honestly, I didn't know how to broach the subject. None of you knew about my sister and I wasn't sure you'd believe me."

They both nodded. Twins were not a topic openly discussed in the Heavens because of the soul issue.

"I understand if you want to banish me," said Shea.

Izzy stood up, clearly agitated. "We're not banishing anyone. I think we should talk to Ash."

"What?" asked Shea.

Meredith stood up also, which forced Shea to stand. "I concur."

"You want to talk to Ash, but he's a demon," said Shea, clearly surprised.

"Do you think of him as such?" asked Izzy.

"No but he's complicated. I wish I could explain how I feel when I'm with him. He did the impossible. He found my twin and saved her and the others."

"The others?" asked Izzy.

"The others," said Ash, materializing in a puff in the prayer room, instantly moving to Shea's side to slip a possessive arm around her middle.

"Why do you keep popping into our lives?" said Izzy, not looking pleased.

"He is the one responsible for possessing Gareth," stated Meredith.

Ash bowed his head. "What is that human song, sorry, not sorry. Gareth was the only way for me to ascertain the safety of my b'iã and as I tried to explain to you before, I'm on your side."

"You mean when you showed yourself in the alley and forced the visions upon me," said Izzy.

"It was the only way you'd listen," said Ash, kissing the top of Shea's head.

"Oh," said Shea, clearly having omitted that truism.

"Wait, did you just say Shea is your b'iã?" asked Meredith.

"We have the blessing of the Mistress. Shea and I are mated."

"Why does this not surprise me one bit? The Mistress has her hands in many things, but what does she have to do with you, as you are a demon?"

"Half-demon," said Ash.

Izzy gave a look to Meredith and Shea watched Meredith walk closer to Ash.

"May I touch you?" asked Meredith.

"To see my future," stated Ash, clearly understanding her desire.

Meredith nodded. Ash held out his hand and Meredith cautiously accepted it. Shea waited like Izzy as Meredith's touch did the trick. Ash was the first to break the contact.

"Some secrets I shall keep to my own," said Ash, stepping back to once again be closer to Shea.

"Not only is Ash Lucifer's son but it appears he is the son of the Mistress."

"What?" said Shea, easing out of Ash's hold.

Izzy placed her hands on her hips. "This is the strangest day I've had in a long time."

"You never mentioned this to me," said Shea to Ash.

"You never asked," he said, giving her one of his dazzling smiles.

"I have a lot more questions racing through my mind but the pressing thing at the moment has to do with Shea's twin."

"Ah, yes, Isis, the new Queen of Hell," said Ash.

"Is she a threat to us?" asked Meredith.

"A good question. I'm not really sure. The bigger question is, is she a threat to your Heaven?"

"Yes," said Shea, quietly, but they all heard.

Izzy had started to pace around the room. "How so?"

"She plans to lead Lucifer's army," said Shea.

"But she's an angel," said Meredith, looking exasperated.

"An angel your precious Heaven discarded and left to rot," said Ash, looking smug.

"It appears as if it's your Heaven too?" said Izzy.

"Oh no, trust me, my upbringing was firmly in Hell and it was nothing like what you could begin to imagine," said Ash.

Shea felt overwhelmed. "This is all my fault."

Ash brought her close to him. "This, my b'iã, is not your fault. If anyone is at fault it's your Almighty."

"Ash, don't say such."

"What, why not? He's the one who said twins can't exist and this one soul notion is ludicrous."

"He is never at fault and our faith remains strong. We will defend our home no matter what. This army we're training is essential. The God of Hell, your father, can't break the Heavenly Gates."

"I concur," said Ash.

"I think we need to hold a meeting with everyone," said Izzy, surprising Shea.

"You would want to disclose this to all my fellow sisters?" asked Shea, looking uncomfortable.

"Izzy, I must insist we think on this. I don't feel it will do any good for our fellow sisters to know about Ash."

"That is the problem, Meredith. We've all been holding our secrets too close to our hearts. We must pray for guidance. Ash obviously can come and go from our home here and we need his help if we're going to defeat Isis army."

"As much as I'd like to offer my help, you must understand my allegiance is still rooted by necessity with my father," said Ash.

"Necessity, I understand but if I understand correctly, you've gained some additional angel powers thanks to

Shea's love and it's made you independent of your father's realm," stated Izzy.

"Correct," said Ash.

"Great. We're going to use you to our advantage. We need a spy in Lucifer's realm and you fit the bill."

Ash placed his hands on his hips. "Izzy, you continually surprise me with your devious thinking. Are you sure you're not part demon?" teased Ash.

Izzy pursed her lips. "Sadly, I'm one hundred percent angel."

Ash tisked. "Fallen angel."

Shea felt the tension in the prayer room. "Ash will do it. He'll be our spy."

"I will?" he said, cocking his head to the side to look at Shea.

"Yes, you will, because I asked you," said Shea, going up on her toes to give his cheek a playful kiss.

He blushed. "Well, for you, anything my b'iã."

"You'll do it?" asked Izzy, needing clarification.

"Yes. I will do as Shea has asked. Now, before I go, I do have one request."

"Why does this not surprise me?" said Meredith.

"It's really a small one but do not attempt to rescue Winter."

"Why not?" asked Izzy.

"You have my word she is fine and will be returned shortly."

"If Ash is giving his word, you can trust him," said Shea, stepping forward.

Izzy moved to the closed door. "It appears at this moment we have to trust you, Ash. I think it best you leave before..."

"Before Zacky comes flying through the door. Yes, I too smell his divine scent," said Ash with a sneer.

I shall see you later in your room, said Ash, privately to Shea.

Shea smiled and then in a flash Ash was gone.

"A demon and an angel mated with the Mistress' blessing. Will wonders never cease? And did anyone know the Mistress had a child? asked Izzy, running a hand through her hair. "For now, we shall keep the confidence of this meeting to ourselves. Shea do not let Ash possess any others and if he must visit keep it strictly to your room."

"You're not planning to tell Nathanael?" asked Meredith, clearly surprised.

"Not at the moment. I need counsel," admitted Izzy.

"You're going to speak with the Mistress?" asked Shea.

"Worse, I'm going to speak with the Mistress' sister, Lilith," said Izzy.

Shea did not like the idea one bit but considering all she'd disclosed to her fellow Cherub sisters she would not be the one to voice dissent.

CHAPTER THIRTY-TWO

A knock on her bedroom door had Meredith bolting awake. Who could it be? The last person, or angel she expected to see was Zachary; yet there he stood, in his splendor asking if he could come in to talk to her.

"In here?" asked Meredith. The intimacy of her bedroom felt like a breach she didn't want Zachary to step into.

"Yes," he said.

"Okay, come in," said Meredith, moving back to allow him to enter. She had a plush mauve two-piece 'Hello Kitty' on and knew it made her look ridiculous but it also was extremely comfortable and soothing. After tonight's demon attack at the Ritz and the disclosure from Shea about Ash, Meredith had craved comfort more than fashion.

"What's up?" asked Meredith, pleased she at least was a neat freak and nothing unmentionable was left hanging about in her bedroom.

"Two things. I know Ash has been here and he's the one I presume who possessed Gareth. Also, I spoke with my father and told him I am relinquishing my claim to the Cherub he's ordered me to wed."

Meredith plopped down on her bed. Zachary never minced words but it was a lot for her to take in. "Why would you tell your father such?"

Zachary surprised her further by coming to kneel at her feet by the bed. "I know you can't forgive me yet but I am sorry I couldn't speak in your defense. Know that my feelings for you have never wavered."

"I..." mumbled Meredith, wondering for a minute if she might be dreaming.

Zachary grasped her hands and the contact woke up every aspect of Meredith.

"Since coming to Earth, I've had my eyes opened. I'm so proud of your strength Meredith and I wish for us to get reacquainted with one another, on the original terms the Oracle ordained."

"I'm sorry, Zachary, I'm not following this."

"I told you, I had to leave and I went home and had a frank discussion with my father and he's agreed it would be best if I not return home."

"Your father kicked you out of the Heavens?" asked Meredith, jumping up from the bed, needing to put much-needed space between her body and Zachary.

Zachary got up and the breadth of him took her breath away. "It's not like he hasn't done so before. My father has a temper and he likes everything to be his way. He will calm down and I shall return on my terms and my terms include you."

"What?"

"I want you to be my b'iã?"

Meredith's whole world tilted. His b'iã; it was a dream come true. But Meredith knew her dreams always got shattered.

Somehow Meredith found her tongue. "Zachary, this is all new to me."

"I know and I understand your reluctance but know I shall woo you."

"Woo me?" Yes, Meredith thought she must have been a parrot in another life.

He approached her and with a gentleness which belied his warrior-honed body, he tipped her face up and then his lips feather-light touched hers. And like before in the Heavens, he made heavenly fire race through her body. Meredith didn't remember her arms reaching up to clutch him tighter, but she felt his arms anchor her to him in a way causing her to sigh in ecstasy. When they finally needed oxygen to breathe they were both flushed and panting from their quick marathon of kissing.

Zachary was the one who stepped back. "I should have thought twice before coming to your personal bedroom to tell you this."

Meredith smiled. Temptation was a sin but for once Meredith longed for it. As if he read her thoughts, Zachary smiled.

"I think it best if I leave. We shall continue this discussion at a more suitable time," said Zachary.

Meredith knew he was correct. Then she recalled his first statement. "How do you know about Ash?"

"Ah, yes, Ash, complicated demon. I've encountered him before."

Now this news did truly surprise Meredith. Clutching a pillow from her bed, Meredith sat on her bed and urged Zachary to have a seat beside her. "Tell me everything you know about him."

"You are not going to like it."

"He's a demon, of course I'm not going to like it."

"He's much more than a mere demon. He's Lucifer's son."

"Well, yes I know and he's the Mistress' son also."

"He is?" asked Zachary.

Meredith nodded. She knew Izzy would disclose everything they'd learned from Shea to Nathanael who in turn would tell Zachary, so revealing their secret didn't feel distasteful.

"Shea is Ash's b'iã. It's why I smelled a demon in the house. He's also the same demon to show Isabella

Lucifer's army. All of this makes me wonder what he's playing at," said Zachary.

"We know we need to watch him, but he's agreed to be a spy for us in Lucifer's realm and the information he can pass our way will help."

"Or will it help him. I do not trust a demon and most certainly not Ash."

"How do you know of him?"

"My first time banished to Earth, as I told you was a learning experience. I was young and naive and thought humans weak and unworthy of the Almighty's love. Ash played into my own weakness to show me things I wish now I hadn't participated in."

"Ash is the demon who saved you?" said Meredith, recalling the tale Zachary had told her of the time humans had tried to end his life and he'd been saved by a demon.

"He nursed me back to health. He never told me his name, but we both knew I knew he was a demon. The black death was purging the humans when I was on Earth and I thought they deserved the wrath of the Almighty. Ash didn't believe such. I was feverish for days but he wouldn't let me die. When I was well, he told me to look at the small things humans do for each other before departing my life for good, or so I thought. I remember thinking he made no sense but I took his words to heart and the more I looked around, the more revelation was revealed. The Almighty was everywhere on Earth. Even with the plague destroying people, and with hunger and fear clawing at most, I witnessed the miraculous. Kindness and love abounded and I had my eyes opened thanks to a demon. I thought I recognized his smell when I entered the brownstone to force the smoke out and now I know why. He's once again in my life."

Meredith was stunned. It was the most she'd ever heard Zachary speak. "He's in all our lives and most importantly, it would appear, in Shea's life for good."

"Now it makes sense why he saved me. If he's truly the son of the Mistress he's also part angel."

"We did mention such and he didn't like the notion one bit."

"I bet he didn't. And we shouldn't. He has leverage now, by claiming Shea's power."

"Yes, there is that but I've been thinking," said Meredith.

"What?"

"Shea too has power. Tonight, when she sang she controlled the demons and I think she's stronger than we know."

"If she's stronger than it's safe to assume Isis, her twin, who is now the new Queen of Hell, could be even stronger."

"A good point, I hadn't thought of," said Meredith, yawning.

Zachary smiled. "You're lovely looking when you're tired."

"I'm a hot mess, as they say," teased Meredith.

"Then I like this hot mess. It's time I leave. I shall see you tomorrow," said Zachary, leaning over to give her a quick kiss on the cheek.

He was gone before she could speak or do something drastic, like pull him into the bed. Most certainly, such could not happen.

Meredith slid back under her covers, fearful with all which had transpired in the last twenty-four hours she'd never get to sleep but she needn't have worried. For the first time in a long time, when Meredith closed her eyes she saw her future and it wasn't full of darkness anymore and for such, she said a blessing of thanks to the Almighty and the Mistress.

CHAPTER THIRTY-THREE

Izzy was beyond tired but she needed answers and to do such, it meant a trip once again to the Doyen's house.

Izzy knocked on the door and Sky answered the door.

"Have you found Winter?" she asked.

"Yes and no. I need to speak with the Doyen," said Izzy, marching into the hall.

"She's in prayer. Where is Winter?"

"That's a bit complicated at the moment but she's safe."

Sky cocked her head to the side. "Safe? By whose measure?"

"Like I said, it's complicated. I've been told she's safe and shall be returned to us."

"By whom?"

Izzy wasn't in the mood for a discussion with Sky and certainly couldn't tell her a demon told her Winter was safe so she sidestepped Sky's worried inquisition. "My task with the Doyen is urgent. I'm sorry Sky but I must see her."

Sky held out her hand indicating the way to the prayer room, not like Izzy needed it, but she appreciated the gesture and the silence of her questions.

Izzy gave a gentle knock on the prayer room door.

"Enter," said the Doyen.

Izzy strolled into the room, willing a calm she didn't feel. They'd tried once before to summon Lilith but to no avail. Now she would have to resort to drastic measures.

"You've found Winter?" asked the Doyen, gracefully moving from her kneeling position to stand.

"We know where Winter is and we've been assured she's safe and shall be returned to us."

"Dare I ask how you obtained this information?"

"It's complicated but more importantly, I'm here, because we must try to summon Lilith again."

The Doyen grimaced. "I don't think she will show herself in your presence."

Izzy thought that as well, but she'd come armed. She held out her hand which contained a small vial filled with blood.

"Should I ask whose blood?"

It was Ash's blood but Izzy wouldn't betray his trust. "Best not to. I'm sure she'll come now."

The Doyen wisely refrained from speaking. She took the vial and then the two of them moved to the center of the room. The Doyen unsheathed a sharp knife, which had been tucked inside her tunic, to slice her palm. She let the blood fall into the bowl and then uncapped the vial and poured the contents into the bowl. Bowing her head, the Doyen spoke what sounded like an enchantment to Izzy, but she knew from previous experience it was the words used to summon Lilith.

Izzy found herself praying, hoping Lilith this time would feel the urge to materialize and grace them with her presence.

It felt like an eternity but then Izzy felt a third presence in the room. When she opened her eyes, the last thing she expected was to see a stunning, beautiful woman, about six feet, with long red tresses, dressed in black leather. She was ageless and sexy. The complete opposite to her sister, the Mistress.

"Why have I been summoned, where is Ash and why in Hell is there an angel standing next to you?"

The Doyen bowed her head. "Lilith, we come in need of aid."

"Only by the grace of Hell have I not departed you to the next world, Doyen. Angel speak, my patience grows weary."

Izzy swallowed. "Ash came to us and informed us there's a new Queen of Hell who plans to form an army to open the Gates of Heaven."

Lilith came closer. It took a lot of willpower for Izzy not to inch back. Lilith's eyes were the color of dark chocolate. "Why would Ash come to you?"

Izzy didn't want to mention his connection with Shea. "You will have to ask him yourself. All I know is he sounded concerned with this new Queen of Hell."

Lilith laughed. "There is only one Queen of Hell; me. What you say is impossible and why are you here in my sacred house?"

"We've been helping them," said the Doyen.

Izzy wasn't one to dispute a legend but Ash hadn't been lying. "I don't mean to displease you but why would Ash lie about a new Queen?"

"Ash was born lying. It's his nature. Lucifer might have a new plaything and she might very well call herself Queen, but only I hold true power. I honestly don't care what Lucifer is planning. I've left his realm for the call of freedom and independence."

Izzy by the blessed light understood her call for freedom but she wasn't about to voice such to Lilith. Opening up to Lilith felt like a betrayal to the Mistress but what option did Izzy have? She needed Lilith to topple the current Queen of Hell. "Is it safe to say you haven't been in Hell recently?" said Izzy.

"Listen little angel, I don't like you. You reek of my sister and I've come to never trust angels," said Lilith. "My whereabouts don't concern you."

"But if the Gates of Heaven fall then won't you lose all your angel powers," said Izzy, trying to push home why they had called Lilith.

"I was kicked out of the Heavens in case you missed that part of your education."

Izzy smiled. "As too were I and my fellow Cherubs."

The news seemed to stun Lilith. "You are a fallen angel?"

"Yes. We were punished for taking up arms to defend our home," said Izzy.

Lilith started to march around the room. "A Cherub holding a sword. It must have called quite a stir in the Heavens."

"A bunch of Cherubs holding swords, actually. We were all kicked out and exiled to Earth and haven't aged a day since our ruin."

"That is the curse leveled at those who fall. I wasn't as young as you when I fell, thank you Hell for that, but I sense still a feeling of devotion in you."

Izzy nodded. "Our home is the Heavens and my fellow Cherubs will do all we can to defend the Gates against Lucifer's army."

"Why?"

"Why what?" asked Izzy.

"Why defend the Gates after all they did to you and your sisters?"

It was the same question Ash had asked and she didn't flinch in her response. "Our hearts are with the Almighty."

Lilith laughed. "You think the Almighty will reinstate you all? Don't speak, I see it plainly written. You have hope to save your fellow fallen sisters but heed me well, your hope is truly lost."

"That may be the case, but if we can stop Lucifer's army we will."

"And what is it you think I can or would do to help you? The Almighty is not a fan of me."

"Ash thought it best you know about the new Queen."

"I bet he did."

It was the Doyen who moved closer to Lilith this time. "While we know we will never be welcome into the Heavens, the daughters of Lilith are devoted to you and we will follow you anywhere."

Lilith looked on with kindness at the Doyen. "Your devotion warms me."

"But if the Gates of Heaven fall to demons, we would not want you to lose your leverage, or your power. If I understand what Izzy is trying to say, is that the case?"

Lilith blinked and then sighed. "Yes, such could be the case. I guess I have been remiss in not visiting my husband of late."

Izzy was about to speak on behalf of Shea's twin sister, Isis, who was calling herself the new Queen of Hell, but Lilith vanished before she could muster a word.

"I think your new Queen of Hell will be toppled," said the Doyen, voicing exactly what Izzy feared.

Not for the first time, she wondered if this had been Ash's plan all along.

CHAPTER THIRTY-FOUR

It was the middle of the night when Shea felt a calling. She looked at the fire, now embers glowing red in the fireplace. She had expected Ash to return to her and worry knotted itself into her heart, which surprised her. In such a short time, he'd come to mean something to her. Shea wasn't entirely sure how to feel about her conditioning, which said she was his b'iã, his mate, for life.

You said you'd visit me, said Isis, speaking on their telepathic link they'd shared as Cherubs.

I have no idea how to get to Hell.

I shall solve your dilemma. Step close to the fire and when you see my hand reach out, grasp it.

But won't I get burned?

Stop thinking one dimensionally. Trust me, you won't be harmed.

Will Lucifer be there?

No. He's gone to deal with some urgent business.

There was a tone in Isis voice which Shea recognized. Her twin was annoyed and sounded slightly jealous.

What are you waiting for?

Isis sounded totally irritated. I'm coming. This is all new to me. Okay, I'm at the fire.

Take my hand.

Shea looked at the fire and sure enough a hand materialized. Saying a prayer and going on a leap of faith, Shea reached out and grasped her twin's hand. Instantly, she fell into a vortex and while she felt heat, she also welcomed its touch. When next she opened her eyes, she blinked.

Hell looked like a palace. The floor, the color of onyx was marble and the suite which had at least ten-foot ceilings, was elegantly decorated with old English furniture, giving it elegance.

"This is Hell?" said Shea, once the feeling of nausea settled. Spinning through a vortex was not for the faint of heart.

"Of course, it's Hell. Not what you expected?"

"No, not at all," said Shea, trying to take it all in.

"It's because Hell is an illusion. Trust me, you wouldn't want to see the real room. Lucifer has no taste and the stench, let's just say you are lucky you can't smell the rot," said Isis, pouring her what looked like an alcoholic drink.

"I can't drink alcohol" said Shea, clearly surprising Isis. "Sorry, it's an angel thing, it doesn't mix well with us."

Isis downed her drink. "Thankfully it doesn't affect me."

"Why did you want to talk?" asked Shea.

"I don't want to hate you. After all, you did send Ash to save me, but we're on opposite sides."

"Only because you've chosen the wrong side," said Shea, finally choosing an elegant blue sofa to sit on.

"Why should the Almighty get my allegiance and my devotion? How could a baby, an innocent, be thrown out of the Heavens?"

"I don't agree with what happened to you or to the others but..."

Isis poured another drink. "You seem to have blind faith and obedience, which feels to me as if you condone what happened to us."

Shea jumped up from the sofa. "Never. What was done was wrong but my love for the Almighty, my home, the Heavens, can't fade."

"Why?"

"Why what?"

"Why can't it fade? Have you never questioned your belief?"

Yes, Shea most certainly had and for a long time she too struggled but her love for the Almighty was steadfast. "This is why you wanted to meet? My faith is strong and I will fight with all I have to keep demons from destroying my home."

"I wish we weren't so dissimilar."

"We will always be linked by birth but maybe we need time to truly get to know each other," said Shea.

Isis gave a nod and was about to say something when Ash materialized in the room.

"Shea, you must leave immediately," said Ash, grasping her arm and hauling her closer to him.

"What, why?"

"Well, it appears Lucifer has returned from his errand."

"Yes, my darling, I have. Now, this is a sight I never thought to see. My own son with, can it be true, yes, it does appear to be, his angel wife," said Lucifer.

Shea tried not to stare but Lucifer, in all his glory, encompassed the room with his height and breadth of body.

"This is my sister I was telling you about," said Isis, moving to place her hand on Lucifer's arm.

"You promised I wouldn't be harmed," said Shea, wishing she'd stayed in bed for the night.

"Father, I can explain," said Ash.

Lucifer didn't wait for an explanation. He blasted Ash with a god-bolt, which forced Ash to his knees. Immediately, Shea screamed. "What are you doing? He's your son."

"A son trying to overthrow me. Do you think I don't know what you've done, and why you secured an angel?" said Lucifer, advancing on Ash.

Shea unfurled her wings, trying to protect Ash from his father's vengeance. It was futile. Shea screamed as the bolts tore through her wings, crippling her.

"You must leave me," said Ash.

Blood steadily dripped down his side and there was no way he could stand. "Never. I will not leave you."

Ash tried to push her away. "You must. I can't bear to watch you die also."

Shea didn't want to die but she knew in her soul, she could not leave her mate. A third blast tore through Shea's shoulder and searing pain almost made her throw up. Mustering what little courage she had Shea started to sing the prayer for help to the one person she could think of; the Mistress.

"You think she'll come and save you," teased Lucifer, getting ready to send another bolt their way.

Shea closed her eyes, bracing for the pain. Unexpectantly she felt heavenly calm descend on her.

"You shall not kill my son," said Lilith, materializing to stand in her glory directly in front of Lucifer.

"I can kill him if I want. He's my son also," said Lucifer, about to throw a bolt. When he let it loose, Lilith stepped into his line of fire and absorbed the blow without a sound.

Lucifer screamed.

Lilith tilted her head and then waved her hand over Ash and Shea. When next Shea opened her eyes they were back in her blessed room. Ash was bleeding like a river. Shea felt helpless but knew she needed help.

"I'll be right back." Shea could barely walk, her wings hurt so much, but she had to secure help from her sisters. Practically falling down the stairs she started yelling for help. Meredith was the first to race out of her room.

"What by the blessed Mistress has happened?" she asked.

"It's Ash. He was badly wounded by his father. I'm worried he's going to die," said Shea, starting to shake.

"I'll send Anya to get Izzy, who's in the training center and we will do all we can to save him but now we must attend to you. You are bleeding everywhere," said Meredith.

"You will save him? But he's a demon," said Shea.

"And he's your mate and you are our sister. We will come to his aid and by the blessing of the Almighty we will pray for his swift recovery. I must get you back to your room to heal," ordered Meredith.

Shea, with Meredith's help, ascended the stairs to her room. Every movement hurt.

"Anya, thank you for coming. Ash needs our help. Can you get Izzy? She's in the training center," said Meredith to Anya, who was walking up the stairs.

"Yes, of course. Should I tell the rest?"

Shea knew the rest were the Seraphims. At this point what does it matter?

"Tell Zachary we might need his vocal powers," said Meredith, surprising Shea and Anya.

"I gather he can sing," said Meredith, taking Shea's arm. "You are going into shock. I am assuming Ash is in your room."

Shea wasn't sure how she found the strength to make it back up the stairs but the sight when she opened her bedroom strengthened her faith.

There stood the Mistress with her arms tightly wrapped around her bloodied son, but the shine of light cascading over them meant one thing; Ash was being made whole.

Shea felt Meredith hauling her down and she realized then she wasn't kneeling or bowing her head so she immediately postulated herself, which considering she was barely standing didn't say much.

"Thank you, Mother," said Ash, stepping out of her embrace.

Something tangible passed between the two but then the Mistress vanished. Izzy ran into the room, almost colliding with both Shea and Meredith.

"He's healed," she said, panting.

A second later Nathanael, Zachary, and Mike stormed into Shea's bedroom. Meredith helped Shea to her feet. Exhaustion poured out of her as she finally fell onto her bed.

"The Mistress healed him," clarified Meredith for everyone.

"What happened?" asked Izzy.

Shea quickly launched into her night; how her sister lured her to Hell, how Lucifer returned and what he did to his son and how Lilith saved Ash.

"Actually, that wasn't Lilith. It was the Mistress masquerading as Lilith," said Ash, shocking them all into silence.

Ash knelt by Shea's bed.

"I thought you might die," she said.

He winked at her. "Can't get rid of me so easily, my b'iã."

"You are the Mistress' son," stated Nathanael, not looking pleased.

"Yes. Until tonight, she never acknowledged her parenthood to me. I thought for the longest time Lilith, who became my step-mother when I was quite young, might be my true mother so you can well imagine my delight and surprise when I discovered the truth," said Ash.

"And tonight, Lucifer wanted to kill you. Why?" asked Izzy.

"Because he knows I'm trying to stop him," said Ash.

"And why would you want to stop him?" asked Nathanael.

"Balance. The realms need such. If Lucifer takes the Heavens, chaos will rule and all humans will die," said Ash, grasping her hand.

"And what is your plan?" asked Zachary.

"Sorry, Shea, but the new Queen of Hell, your twin, must vacate the realm."

"I've spoken with Lilith and I do believe she shall take care of it," stated Izzy, causing alarm to flare to life for Shea.

"I don't want my sister harmed," said Shea, attempting to pull out of Ash's hold.

"I wish I could say that wasn't on Lilith's agenda but she left before I could voice such. Lilith understands this balance you speak of, Ash. Will your father take Lilith back?"

Ash laughed. "Yes. She's a pull he hates and loves at the same time. Her pull, as you well know, is her angel power."

"But doesn't Isis have power also?" asked Meredith.

"No. Lucifer gave a part of himself to make her live, which doesn't give him more power."

"You're saying he'll toss my sister aside for Lilith?" asked Shea, getting more agitated.

"If we're lucky that's all he'll do."

"And if we're not?"

"He'll eliminate your sister," said Ash.

Shea had enough of everyone plotting to destroy her sister. She was exhausted beyond belief but also felt adrenaline course through her veins. "I'm sorry but I need everyone to leave my room. I need time to think," she said, to the crowd of people still in her bedroom.

They all understood and nodded as they left. Izzy gave her hand a tight squeeze of support as she made her exit.

Left in her room with only Ash, Shea turned to him. "You must help me save her."

"What I must do now is heal you. It's killing me knowing you are in such pain." Ash scouted up on the bed and then leaned his head toward her. The kiss was gentle and yet so much more. The power that fueled through her caused Shea to arch up off the bed as a heat soared into the marrow of her bones.

"Thank you," said Shea, once he finished kissing her properly.

"It is always my pleasure to kiss you. What you did was foolish. No more saving me."

"I could no more let you die then stop breathing. It is not in my nature."

"I feel unworthy of your trust and faith."

Shea, fully healed, reached up to cup Ash's face. "My faith in you sustains us both, however, I beg of you to save my twin."

"I knew you'd ask this of me," he said, smiling as he pulled her to his form. "I have a plan but you might not like it."

"If it will save Isis, I will," said Shea, fearing she'd saved her twin once but might not be able to a second time.

CHAPTER THIRTY-FIVE

Ash had known Shea would ask him to save her twin sister. After all, she'd been saving Isis for her entire life by going without food so that the scrapes of substance left on her plate would be given to her twin. Isis, might not confess to this, but Ash had talked to enough of the other twins to know this was the case for them all. Their existence had been tethered directly to their twin. If their twin acknowledged them and made the sacrifice they managed to continue to live.

"You must ask the Mistress for a favor," he said.

Shea looked like she'd swallowed nails. "Why would she assist me?"

She shaped your fate and my destiny with her faith, thought Ash. "Has she ever denied the fallen help?"

Shea laughed, but not in a funny way. "She allowed the Council to exile us from our home."

"Maybe she had a purpose," said Ash.

"Purpose? You must be kidding me."

"Think for a moment. If you hadn't been exiled, we wouldn't have met. And she did save us both from Lucifer's realm."

Her eyes softened. "I am by the blessed light happy to never set foot in your father's realm ever again. And I don't regret meeting you."

Ash shivered. He didn't want Shea to hate his realm but for now remained silent.

"It's because you've fallen for my charm and my body," he said, grinning playfully.

A blush crept up Shea's face. "I am not admitting to such."

"You don't need to; it's written all over your face and obviously in the Heavens." Ash took Shea's hand. "Ask her. All she can say is no and then we'll deal with it."

"But what exactly am I asking her for?"

"You're asking her to wipe your sister's memories, all of them. She needs to believe she's an ordinary human and then she'll be safe."

"Wipe her memories...but then she'll forget about me."

"But she'll live and you won't forget about her. There is a difference. I am not kidding in my fear for her health. Lilith will enjoy torturing her."

Shea blanched. "But forgetting she's an angel, what about her being part demon?"

"I shall take care of everything," said Ash.

"How?"

"Nothing you need to worry about but it can be done. Now, I must go back to my realm. Call the Mistress to you and plead your request."

"How will I let you know if it succeeds?"

"Oh, I'll know. Now, before I depart, I would ask, no I'm begging for a kiss."

"There isn't time for a kiss," said Shea.

Ash pulled her closer and then swooped in for a heated kiss. Shea didn't resist. She tugged him closer. "There is always time for a kiss. I must leave you but have faith in your request."

Shea nodded but Ash knew she was worried. He didn't blame her. Speaking directly to the Mistress was not for the faint of heart. Casting one last look at his b'iã, Ash placed his hands over the fire and a second later the heat of Hell took him to his realm.

Ash didn't waste time. He dematerialized and let his molecules take him to the furthest reaches of Hell. There in the pit of Hell, a place no one wanted to walk into, let alone visit was the thing he thought never to see again– Lucifer's brother's heart, entombed in the rivers of despair. The heart magically entombed in a gold box hadn't shriveled up, rather it kept its blood red color. The river of despair was a molten lava river with currents, tides and a nature as unpredictable as his father. Ash knew if he could get his hands on the heart, he could ensure Lilith would not harm Isis and more importantly his destiny would start aligning with the purpose, as the Mistress had eloquently stated.

The question was how to reach into the river to secure the heart.

"What are you doing here?" asked Kali, coalescing into her solid form beside him.

"Visiting a relation."

"A what?"

"A relation," said Ash, barely resisting rolling his eyes.

Kali looked out at the river. "You mean the old gross heart, which father claims is his brother's heart."

Ash started pacing by the river. "Yes. Don't you ever wonder about him?

"Can't say I've given him much thought. He sounded weak," said Kali.

Ash started to pace by the river. Weak! The urge to throttle his sister once again took hold, but Ash wisely curbed his natural instinct. "Why are you following me?"

"I thought you might like to know, Winter has left."

Ash turned to look at his sister. "You like her?"

Kali shrugged. "She was not what I expected, and..."

"And what?" asked Ash.

"Rumor has it my mother is returning."

"Well, this news must make you happy," said Ash, still trying to figure out how to get the heart.

"I guess. I'm also wondering what her game is."

That's right, be smart, Kali, thought Ash. "I'm sure we'll all find out soon enough."

"Don't you find it odd, all these decades later, she finally decides to show up only when a new Queen of Hell has declared herself?"

"Guess she missed our father dear," said Ash, flippantly.

"Or, maybe someone alerted her to the fact Lucifer had found someone else."

"Could be," said Ash.

"I'm not sure how I feel about this, Ash," said Kali. "And exactly why are you pacing along this river bed?"

Ash sighed. "I need his heart."

Kali grimaced. "You need our dead uncle's heart. Why?"

"Leverage and before you ask more, I can't and won't tell you."

Kali cocked her head to the side. "Even if I help you, you won't tell me."

Okay, Ash hadn't seen that coming. His sister helping him. Did Hell freeze over? "You're asking me to trust you when you seem to be father's right hand."

"I thought that's what he assigned to you."

Ash grinned. "Let's be clear. If I let you help me, you must promise to never tell him."

"I promise."

Ash wasn't buying it but he needed her help. "Do you still have your sword you dipped in hellfire?"

Kali nodded.

"Conjure it up to you."

"Start talking, Ash. What's this all about?"

"I need father diverted for a bit and stealing his brother's heart will do the trick."

"Or it will drive him over the edge."

"Yes, but by then, Lilith will be here to keep him sane."

Kali marched over to him and poked him hard. "You knew she was coming back?"

"I wasn't entirely sure, but I did suspect."

"Could it be because either you told her about Isis or had someone do your dirty work for you?"

"Maybe," said Ash, with a wink.

Kali looked like she wanted to inflect some serious damage to him.

"You're up to something Ash, but I will help."

Kali conjured the sword and then Ash unfurled his wings. "Okay, you're going to have to... wait, what are you doing?"

"Getting the blasted heart," said Kali, flying over the object. She used the sword to nudge it toward the shore and only once it was within reach did Ash grasp it.

"Thank you, Kali."

"No, thank you, Ash. My mother and I have some unfinished business to discuss."

Ash nodded and then quickly flashed himself out of the Hell realm and back to Earth. The only safe place to store the heart, encased in a gold box, with a clear cover, was in the fallen angels' brownstone. Checking to ensure Shea wasn't in her room, he rematerialized and then used a demon spell to ensure no demon or angel could discern the heart's location. Only then did Ash will himself back to his father's domain knowing he'd have to soon put on the best performance of his life.

CHAPTER THIRTY-SIX

The night was fading to dawn and Shea knew she was stalling. She wasn't sure of her destination until she found her feet once again at the Jewish Center. Unlocking the doors, she strolled through the building, knowing any security tapes would short-circuit as she walked close. When she got to the library, she took out her knife and on her knees, head bowed in reverence she cut her palm and spoke the pleading words for a visitation from the Mistress.

"You have called me forth twice in one day" said the Mistress, standing directly in front of Shea.

"By your blessed grace thank you for answering my call."

"Speak, my child by the grace of the Almighty."

Shea swallowed. "I ask a favor of thee."

"Saving your life wasn't enough? This favor you speak of is not for you?"

"Thank you once again for saving me and Ash. But I wish you to take my twin sister's memories from her of me, of what she is, so she can live a normal life as a human."

Silence filled the library. Finally, Shea dared to raise her eyes.

The Mistress, veiled in her usual black heavy robes seemed to be calculating the request. "I beg of thee for I fear Lilith..."

"What of Lilith?"

"I fear Lilith means to harm my sister."

"Rise, and come to me, child."

With trembling legs, Shea did as asked. Standing next to the Mistress, on equal footing so to speak, felt sacrilegious.

"I have need of your hand," said the Mistress.

"My hand?" asked Shea.

"What I ask of you is your faith and for such I need your hand."

Shea did as instructed and held out her hand. When the Mistress went to remove her black glove, she said quickly. "Close your eyes."

Shea quickly closed her eyes. Heat the likes of which she'd never known fired through her hand, body and soul the minute the Mistress made contact with her flesh. Shea wasn't sure how long they were clasped but when she finally could reclaim herself, she took a shuddering breath to clear herself.

"I will do as you ask. Your fate is sealed and your path not an easy one, but already destiny is walking with you and Ash. Your faith is steadfast. I shall grant your request."

Immediately, Shea fell to her knees and bowed her head in reverence. "Thank you, Mistress, thank you."

When Shea looked up, she was alone, but for the first time in a long time she smiled. The Mistress would take care of her sister. Ash was right. She might be sad her sister wouldn't know of her existence but the alternative was something she could never live through.

Shea quickly walked back home to the brownstone, mulling over the Mistress' words. What did she mean by destiny walking with her and Ash? Only when she was secure in her bed, with the light of dawn streaming through a small part within the curtains, did Shea truly fall asleep.

She dreamt. Strange dreams where she could hear her name being called. She walked by an elegant lady who held a child's hand. She watched them laughing as they fed the swans in the Public Garden. She couldn't see the child but a sense she knew the lady had her squirming in her bed.

"I've got you," said the voice, and somehow, some instinctive part of Shea knew Ash was holding her.

When much later she woke, dark had once again stealed through the day.

"Did I sleep the entire day away?" she asked, feeling still sluggish.

"I'm afraid you did. I told your worried sisters you needed to rest. Nayla just brought you supper about ten minutes ago and I'm sure it's still hot," said Ash, climbing out of bed.

"I asked her and she said yes," said Shea, sitting up in her bed.

Ash smiled. "Yes, I know."

"You know? How?"

"The Mistress asked for my help in securing Isis from my father's realm."

"Is she safe?"

"Completely," said Ash, bringing her the supper tray.

"I want to see her."

"You don't, trust me," said Ash, faking a pout.

"No, I just have a need to see her."

"The terms of the contract are sealed, Shea. She won't know of you."

"But where is she and how will she live as a human?"

"I do not know but she is safe. Now eat, my b'iã," said Ash, feeding her bits of the soft bread, made from Nayla's skillful hands.

Shea didn't realize how hungry she was until she had devoured all her supper.

"I do believe that's the most I've seen you eat," said Ash, smiling.

"I can't believe how hungry I was," replied Shea. "Now, I'm going to take a shower and go to the prayer room."

"The prayer room...and here I had been thinking we would indulge ourselves here," said Ash, playfully patting the bed.

Shea smiled. "Is such all you think about?"

"Yes, when I am with you. But if you have a need for prayer, I will not stop you."

Shea leaned over and kissed Ash. "Thank you."

Ash removed her tray and then helped ease her out of bed, or was he really helping, thought Shea as he kept stealing kisses.

"I won't be long," said Shea, opening the door to her bathroom.

"I have to return to my realm to check on my sister. Enjoy your time in the prayer room and do think fondly of me," said Ash, a minute before he changed into smoke to dash through the fire back to Hell.

Shea wasn't sure she'd ever get used to his party trick. She walked into the bathroom, flicked on the light, unleashed her robe, turned on the shower and when she turned and looked at the mirror, did a double take.

Wiping steam off the mirror, she realized her eyes must have been playing tricks on her. For one moment, as she looked at herself in the mirror, it had seemed as if she'd been pregnant. With her heart beating extra fast, Shea thought what a ridiculous notion. She knew exactly what she and Ash had been doing meant procreation but she was an angel and he a half-demon, so the thought a child could come of their union, had honestly never entered her mind before. With the scent of vanilla-soap filling her senses, Shea looked at her flat belly, praying a prayer as old as time. By the grace of the Almighty, let me not be pregnant.

Shea knew the Almighty liked miracles and children. For the first time the words spoken by the Mistress took on an entirely different meaning.

EPILOGUE

"**Y**ou took your sweet time as usual," said Lilith to her sister, the Mistress.

"I was detained in prayer," said the Mistress, forming beside Lilith.

Lilith sat on her bike; a Street Rod Harley Davidson motorcycle and made a gagging sound in her throat. Her bike was red and black, two of her favorite colors. They were on the pedestrian walkway on the Chelsea Street bridge and it was close to dawn. In another hour Boston would wake up with shifts of humans tending to routine as they scuttled to work.

"So, the angel who dared to take my throne is off limits to me, is such what you are not voicing, sister of my blood?" said Lilith.

The Mistress turned away from Lilith, ever the bane of her existence. "Yes. She is off limits."

Lilith was chewing bubble gum, a horrible sweet invention created by humans. She had dressed exactly how she'd been decades ago, clad in black leather which outlined every curve of her body. Time had stopped for Lilith but the same could not be said for the Mistress, but she kept her secret to herself. Her traditional black robe and veil kept her hidden from her sister's piercing gaze.

Lilith blew a big bubble, knowing her actions infuriated her sister. "Fine. Have it your way. I will need to make it look like I've killed her, or else Lucifer won't buy it."

The Mistress knew this. "You will need this," she said, forming a sword in her hand.

"Oh, nice and shiny, the way I like them," said Lilith taking the sword.

"You need to dip it in hellfire to kill the demon part of Isis."

"And I thought my day couldn't get any better. I'm going to enjoy this."

"Ensure the results are to the contract; she will live as a human."

"By scripture, I'd rather die than live like a human. Are you sure I shouldn't give her a choice?"

"No. Play your part and get her out of Hell. I will take care of her life on earth."

"And what of your son, Ash?"

"Leave him to me," said the Mistress. There was an audible pause in the conversation. They watched a few lights flicker on across the river as day started to assert its dominance. "Why did you leave him?"

"I was bored. All the killing, endless torture, it's the same thing, day in and day out. He's so overbearing and he thinks he's right in everything. I needed to leave," said Lilith, placing the sword on her back.

"And will you stay when you go back?"

"What's with all the questions, sister. Are you missing him?"

The Mistress shuffled closer. "There was a time he wasn't as you describe him."

Lilith got back on her bike and ran a loving hand over the throttle. "Eons ago and another lifetime. He's changed as well you know. All he quests for is power. It truly grows tiresome. However, as you decreed to me at the beginning, we all have our parts to play. Today, I will hold the balance."

"You need to get him to not fight us," said the Mistress.

Lilith smiled. "You know I have a feeling a shift is taking place in your Heavens."

"My home, is thy home."

Lilith laughed. "You can cut scripture speak. It's only your Heaven as well you know. I did your bidding and got kicked out."

"I never asked you."

"You did and you know it. When you told me of what befell you, you knew I'd take care of him, when you couldn't or should I say, wouldn't."

"I had a role to play," said the Mistress, clasping her hands together.

Lilith knew her sister was annoyed and she grinned. It was always hard to get a reaction from her but tonight she'd scored. "As it would appear so do I. But don't think for one moment I don't know what you did."

"The Oracle said..."

"I don't want to hear it," said Lilith.

Together they stood, close, but not daring to touch each other as they looked out over the Boston harbor. The moon, obscured by clouds, was cleaved in half.

"Thank you," said the Mistress.

Lilith peered at her sister. For a second, Lilith thought she'd glimpsed a sheen of unfallen tears in her sister's eyes, hidden behind the mesh cloak.

"Someday, Lucifer will discern the truth of what you did to his brother."

"I fear the day is fast approaching, but for now, Ash and his legacy must remain safe."

"I tried my best with him but..."

"He has a will like his father," said the Mistress.

Lilith heard the barest whisper of vulnerability.

"And how fares Kali?"

"She is a mini-me."

"In such case, I will double the guards on the Gates," said the Mistress.

Lilith chuckled. "Sister of mine, I am reminded, sometimes you are funny."

The Mistress bowed her head. "I often wish our roles had been different."

"We could have done what your beloved fallen angels did," said Lilith, lifting the kick stand on her bike.

"What?"

"We could have fought for our independence from the scriptures and the Oracle and carved our own path," said Lilith, not caring that mockery might commence from her sister for the longing in her voice.

The Mistress sighed. "Destruction was such a path, as you well know."

Lilith said nothing. It had all been said before. "Time for me to go."

The Mistress remained quiet. Silence was a welcoming truce that Lilith was used to.

Lilith started the bike and a second later darted down the pedestrian walkway, not caring that the action was illegal. She drove fast and hard.

The Mistress did not envy her sister's life and prayed for forgiveness.

"The beginning of the new dawn is rising, and I ask for guidance," said the Mistress, fearing what had been foretold since the beginning.

The path for Armageddon had been heralded with the birth of the Heavens but the Mistress would do all within her power to stop the Oracles' hands from winning. If it meant manipulation of her fallen angels to set things right in the realm, she would do what must be done. She'd done the hardest of tasks centuries ago, when she'd first slept with Lucifer's brother. Then in the guise of Lilith she had slept with Lucifer and birthed Ash, the son of the God of Hell, only to hand him over to her blood sister for safe keeping. Yes, she'd never asked such of her sister, but she too knew the power of the role she had to play.

Destiny could not be skirted by even the mightiest of angels, or demons as she'd come to painfully discern. The test her fallen angels must endure was a sacrifice they must yield to for the greater good of the Almighty.

Don't miss all the action from book one, Salvation. Catch up on how these fallen angels came to Earth. Buy Salvation today!

So, these were the teens who had dared to take up arms and lead the heavenly charge against the demons pounding on Heaven's gates. Knowing that sped up his heart because without a doubt these Cherubs were like none he'd ever seen or envisioned.

The hush in the center grew. Nathanael became acutely aware of his own ragged breathing. Nathanael eyed the lead Cherub. She wasn't wearing anything remotely angelic. His heart leapt, eager for the sound of her heavenly voice.

A bell rang, a second and third. A soft, haunting melody of a hum started, growing louder with each Cherub until the girl at center stage, threw her head back and sang. The wail of the sorrow-filled song crashed through every fiber of his being, but the seductive tenor also teased the audience.

There, standing at center stage, was the Cherub who had rescued him two days ago. Then she had taken on the demon-infested humans with deadly throwing stars. Tonight, she stroked each person's soul, allowing the purity of her voice to work its magic, easing their anxiety, allowing them in this moment to let their heart truly love, and feel the power of her heavenly lyrics. The sexy sound traveled through Nathanael's bones.

Every cell in Nathanael's Seraphim body recognized the sensual lilt and the foreign words she sung. Ancient Hebrew, the cadence rolled off her tongue like the taste of heavenly red wine. She flirted with the crowd, who were oblivious to the sexual meaning of her words. Her words caused the fine hairs on his skin to rise with pleasure. If he'd had his wings they'd be arched back, proudly displayed. Shaking his head, Nathanael forced his body to cool, taking another dreaded sip of his drink, wanting the bitter tang, anything to force his mind to heel from the fantasy he was envisioning. When the remaining Cherubs threw their voices into the melody of the song, a flood of such intense love slammed into him, he felt like he'd had one too many urdal—the blessed seeds from the heavenly plant many Seraphim chewed to experience a more divine holy prayer.

Nathanael worked his way through the crowd. A few people he shouldered out of the way until he was close enough to the right of the stage to lean against the wall and watch. A total of four more songs followed.

By the end of their first set his breathing was labored, his heart pounded loudly in his chest and his palms were sweaty.

He moved from the wall to flex his muscles. A part of him was angry. However, he wasn't sure if that emotion was directed at himself or the teens on stage.

What he'd witnessed felt sacrilegious and it burned through him. Glad he'd taken on the mission to extract his future heavenly wife he prayed that tonight he'd be back in heaven's realm. The minute he found her, he'd call to the

Mistress and as promised she'd let them back into the heavenly realm, once his Cherub to be wife agreed to the wedding. Then he'd repent for the impurity of his thoughts. Again, he shifted, wishing his jeans weren't so tight as he tried to calm his emotions.

He prayed one of these Cherubs wasn't Isabella. He didn't want her to be openly displaying her body or voice for mankind. Cherub angels were purity. They exemplified all the heavenly descriptions of what that word entailed.

Marching toward the back of the stage, he wondered why no one stopped him. Cherub angels were never unescorted in the heavens yet here on earth they walked about alone, vulnerable.

A sharp steel blade cut into his throat, catching him off guard.

"Well, what do we have here? Why I do believe it's a Seraphim and just my luck, the one I saved from the alley the other night. To whom do we owe the pleasure of addressing?"

The feel of his own angelic blood sliding down his throat caused Nathanael to attempt to move back. The blade cut more into his flesh, making it painfully obvious the Cherub with the sharp knife wouldn't think twice about ending his existence. Casting aside his anger and stupidity, he recognized he was intrigued by these Cherub teens with their macho-Sera attitudes.

"I am Nathanael, First Born of the House of Raphael."

A gasp stole through the other three angels but not the one controlling the knife.

"Why, Sere, are you here on earth?"

Contempt and hatred spilled from the voice, which only moments before had had him almost on his knees, heart fluttering wildly in reverence. The knife was held expertly in the hand of the band's lead singer.

"I am here to find Isabella and bring her home," he said.

"Why?" the leader asked.

"She is to be my future heavenly wife and I have come to claim her."

"Like hell," she said, twisting around to confront him face to face.

Demon daggers looked more inviting than the leader's pale blue eyes as they narrowed in hatred. Her jaw clenched shut so hard he heard the click of her teeth, as her knife cut deeper into his throat causing more of his golden-hued life essence to flow down his throat onto his collar.

Buy Salvation today and don't miss any of the fallen angel action.

Coming soon book three, **Revelation, Fallen Angel series, Book III:**

Nayla did not like snow. The calendar had declared it was spring two days ago but mother nature was evil. She'd heard the sleet slam into her window with the wind howling through the multitude of cracks gracing the brownstone and had shivered through the night. She did not want to move from the comfort of her ultra-thick duvet, a gift from Anya who knew how much the cold bothered Nayla. However, if she didn't rise, nor too would the bread. Funny how her mother's sayings haunted her more in exile. Not so comical was how easily she'd stepped into her mother's role to become the cook for her sisters. At first, she'd taken on the task because they'd all had duties to fill, but lately something tugged at her for more.

Her mother's whispered conversation while she'd been in the prison awaiting the sentence from the Heavenly Septuagint Council—the thirteen-members who had banished all of them to Earth, still cut her raw.

She would never find the truth of her mother's mission is she stayed in the kitchen. Maybe that was why she'd initially sought refuge as the cook. Being the cook meant a task tethering her to the home, to the kitchen, to the needs of others; all without allowing her true thoughts of why she'd first joined Izzy's fight for independence to reclaim her. Now, here she was feeling trapped with a secret she couldn't divulge.

Nayla shook off her thoughts and slipped out of bed. She pushed her feet into the Hello Kitty slippers Meredith had bought for her and wiggled her toes. Turning on the bathroom light she walked past the mirror and then did a double-take and screamed.

What by the blessed Almighty happened to me?

Anya, her closest sister in the bedroom next door ran into her room. They looked at each other and screamed in unison. Next followed, Izzy and Meredith, both armed with their Kita swords, who looked from Anya and Nayla, with perplexed expressions. Shea stood quietly in the door jam.

"Now this is interesting," said Shea, a smile tugged at the corners of her mouth.

"What has happened to us?" asked Anya, pushing Nayla out of the way so she could observe her reflection in the bathroom mirror.

"I have no idea," said Izzy.

"Nor I," echoed Meredith.

"I think I might know," said Keira, surprising all the sisters, as she stepped fully into Nayla's bedroom.

Keira, the linguist in the group, now had a bright purple mark covering half her face and her traditional straight blonde hair was now curly and dark auburn. She did not push her way to seek her reflection. Nayla wondered if she'd already noticed the change in her own bedroom.

As it was, Nayla was fairly certain she'd lost her mind. When she looked at her reflection gone was the stilted plain blonde Cherub. In her place a dark-skinned young woman, with ebony colored-hair naturally curly which fell half-way down her back, stared back in defiance. Her cheekbones were high and defined. The only thing the same were her eyes; cerulean blue. She looked like a stranger but there was a keen sense of familiar recognition which shook Nayla's soul.

"Please explain what is going on? Are we being tested?" asked Anya, who now had skin alabaster white, with thick straight black hair the same length as Nayla's. She looked like a Japanese princess, with beautiful light brown almond-shaped eyes. Both of them had gained at least two inches in height. Why that knowledge made Nayla want to giggle mystified her.

"I can see better," said Anya, surprising everyone as her smile radiated through the room. "I'm not wearing my glasses. I can see you all and you are not blurry. I think I can handle this."

Anya hadn't needed glasses until she'd fallen from grace and the thick eyeglasses were the only thing allowing her to read her precious books. Not having to rely on them would most certainly be a blessing, thought Nayla.

"You both look so beautiful," said Keira, wistfully.

No one knew what to say to Keira. She took a quick glance at the mirror in Nayla's bathroom and gently touched the purple birthmark. It was on the tip of Nayla's tongue to say, "So do you," but lies weren't in her angel nature.

"I once discovered an ancient script, written in a form of archaic scripture, in the Heavenly library which shocked me. It made reference to the glamour of the Heavens. Now, I understand it," said Keira.

"I wonder if that's like the glamour in Hell," said Shea.

Izzy urged them all to sit on Nayla's bed. "How does the glamour in Hell work?"

"When I was in their realm, it was clear those with power could wield the room to look as they wished. I didn't think it could be
the same for angels but if I think about it, I guess that makes sense."

"I'm not sure I understand," said Meredith.

Like Izzy, she didn't sit. Instead, she turned her back to the group and kept watch out the window.

"The script I found made reference to a time before the glamour in the Heavens when all were unique and different and how a disquiet came to the realm and the Council decided sweeping conformity was what was needed," said Keira.

"What you are saying is that all we viewed in the Heavens was a falsehood," stated Izzy, who had started to pace, clearly
agitated.

Isn't most of the Heavens a falsehood? Nayla wisely kept her mouth shut. She cast her eyes to Shea and like she read her mind; her fellow sister blessed her with a tiny wink.

"The more time spent in Earth's realm the more I feel like our blessed Heavens has many flaws," said Shea.

"Earth has flaws too," said Meredith, quickly, always one to defend her homeland.

"Yes, but a glamour so we all look the same. Sorry, but I can't see how diversity is a bad thing. I always thought we were all so boring and it's good to know at our core, we're all unique. Isn't that what you preached for us, Izzy?" asked Shea.

Before Ash, Lucifer's demon son, had come into Shea's life, she'd been meek and mild, never one to question or stand out. Nayla thought it lovely how all that had changed for Shea. It had taken awhile, but Shea had found her voice and strength and she no longer meekly followed anyone. Nayla loved her more for her conviction. After the incident, which none of them discussed, Shea had lost her blonde locks. She had black hair with a white streak running in the middle, making her look as exotic as Nayla now felt.

"Shea is right. This is not a bad thing. This is a blessed gift. The glamour, or whatever it is, has been lifted for us. I can't imagine the emotions you are all feeling and I do wish I could tell you to take the day to yourselves but alas we must continue our daily training exercises.

Nate told me last night they'd heard from the Earth-born Seraphim's that more humans had been turned into demons. Now is not the time for us to let our guard down. Since we're all up, let's have a quick breakfast and I will meet everyone in the training room in one hour," said Izzy.

Nayla realized Izzy and Meredith hadn't changed in appearance or attitude.

"I can whip up some pancakes," said Nayla, stepping into her role when she wished once again to slink back under her duvet.

Izzy pulled Nayla in for a hug. "We shall fend for ourselves. Get dressed for fighting."

"Thank you," said Nayla. The thought of stepping into the kitchen when she wanted only to touch her skin, feel her kinky curly hair, made her feel nauseous.

Izzy made sure to hug each of the transformed sisters before marching out of the room. Anya followed shortly after and then Keira and Shea. Meredith was the last. She stood rooted to her spot by the window.

"Are you alright, Meredith?" asked Nayla.

Meredith finally turned. She had unshed tears in her eyes.

"I knew of this but could say naught. I detest my curse. I'm so sorry but none of what I saw made sense. What's the good of seeing the future when you can't decipher the meaning?"

Nayla took Meredith's hands in hers, which was a complete role reversal for them. "We all have our curses and none are easy to live with. Never in a million years did I envision this and while Izzy would like us all to pretend it's another normal training day, even she knows, that is not the case. I know she's trying her best with distraction but this skin I'm now wearing feels so unfamiliar. I can't get my head around what Keira has imparted to us. None of it makes sense. How is all of us looking the same a good thing?"

"I have no answers, as usual. Nayla, there's more. I think the path ahead of you is not going to be easy. Please come to me anytime. I will try my best to help."

Nayla removed her hands from Meredith's. *Does she know about my mother's sin?* "Of course, Meredith."

"Now, let's go and find out what the young woman across the street wants with us?" said Meredith, surprising Nayla.

"What?"

"She's been watching the house all morning, which is why I've been at the window. I think we're about to have a visitor."

No sooner did Meredith say the words then the old electrical doorbell buzzed, a sound as piercing as the screams which had earlier graced the house.

Salvation

Fallen Angel Series, Book One

She accidentally cursed them all. He's ready to become the next big thing. Could joining together be the key to their salvation?

Izzy can't find peace. When demons gatecrash the Heavens, the independent Cherub despairs in the face of her mother's death. But the hits keep coming when she tries to fight back, only for her all-girl angel army to get exiled... as permanent teens.

Nathanael has battled as close to the top as possible. With his skills obscenely outweighing his status and locating his soulmate the only way left to advance, the proud Seraphim resolves to meet his destined partner on Earth. The last thing he expects upon arrival is for sparks to fly with a banished Cherub. After Nathanael binds the unconventional beauty to him, he hopes her loud disapproval will be a minor interruption to their destiny.

Dismayed when one of her fellow fallen angels disappears, Izzy cautiously teams with the cocky warrior to reunite her broken sisterhood.

Will the winged rebels return home arm-in-arm, or not at all? Can Izzy convince Nathanael it's up to them to stop a demon army from once again invading the Heavens?

Salvation is the first book in the Fallen Angel YA fantasy series. If you like immortally interesting characters, steamy scenes, and pulse palpitating action, then you'll love Renee Pace's fallen angel series.

Coming Soon... Revelation
Fallen Angels Series Book III

Exiled to Earth with her fellow Cherub sisters because they dared independence, Nayla has kept a secret for years while adjusting to Earth. The Veil, which cloaked all Cherubs in a look of uniformity, has been lifted, but the timeline for all the realms is shifting.

For the first time Nayla sees herself as she was meant to be – a stunning black woman. No longer content to stay in the kitchen, Nayla tackles the pledge she gave her mother; finding her lost brother. The last thing Nayla needs is to fall in love with a human. The sins of her mother will not befall her.

Lucifer teams up with the Fey and demons start possessing the homeless who kidnap human babies to be transformed into slaves for his army. Discovering her brother sets Nayla on a path not foretold. Reclaiming her identity and her family unwittingly means a sacrifice. Can she give up her family and set them on a deadly one-way mission to stop the Fey and Lucifer?

These fallen angels still sing for their supper, but now must stop the path of the apocalypse from claiming three realms.

Chosen by the Sea
A Siren's Lure series, Book One

I drowned and something happened to me. One minute I thought I was dead and the next, I turned into a mermaid. None of it makes sense. My parents won't talk about the incident and my mom's got me popping anti-psychotic pills in the hope of making me forget. I can't forget. I've changed. My parents don't understand. When I died and became a mermaid, something called to me in the sea and I'm trying every day to ignore that summons.

I've got enough on my plate. High school sucks big time and since the incident if I touch someone, I can sense their thoughts so I'm wearing my goth attire which keeps everyone away. Everyone except Ash, a teenage heartthrob hallucination who became real and is now enrolled in my school, and who keeps telling me I'm a long-lost siren princess. Right!

Strange things start to happen; first my parents get kidnapped, Ash tells me he's my protector and I'm not sure that's a good thing and the new Captain of the Hockey team wants to be more than friends.

My life feels out of control. I might not know who or what I am anymore, but I will do anything to free my parents and if that means forcing myself back into the cold Atlantic waters, I vow not to fail them. Between juggling learning high school math, which almost makes me want to kill someone, it's now a race against time as I learn how to control my newfound powers before an evil Sea Witch destroys my family while seizing control of all the Seas.

Then again if my mother's right and this is a psychotic episode, I'm hoping I'll wake up with legs instead of a tail.

Nitty Gritty Series:
Off Leash: How a Dog Saved My Life
Nitty Gritty Series, Book One

"Off Leash is a gritty, uncompromising, heart-wrenching, *real* read that will prey on your mind for weeks after you've read it." – Kiwi, Amazon Reviewer

The chips are down for Jay Walker. Life was throwing curve balls at him long before he hit his teen years but now things are piling up. His mother is out of control and the one person who he loves with all his heart, his sister, is sick. Desperate for money to keep his family together, Jay takes a dog walking job, never suspecting how quickly this one act will change his life.

Ollie's life lately has become the cage. At first when another dog walker enters his life, Ollie lets him know who's boss; after all, another teen walking him doesn't mean anything. The last thing Ollie expects is to develop a fierce protectiveness toward Jay. There's something about the young boy which resonates and touches Ollie. When Jay takes Ollie home, he meets the little sister, who is ill and sees another side to the silent teen. Ollie quickly understands his mission in life – his role is to protect Jay at all costs.

As two unlikely strangers, a dog and a young teen, develop their friendship more obstacles get thrown into their path. Ollie will step into the role of guard dog to rescue Jay while Jay struggles to keep the people he loves safe.

Funny how the person you end up counting on and willing to place your life on the line for isn't at all who you expect. This is a poignant story about a young boy entering turbulent teenage years who discovers when every other person lets you down, a dog's love can keep you going.

Check out Off Leash book trailer at http://youtu.be/8TlPncNAzNQ

Amazon Breakthrough Novel Finalist

Off Limits: How a Friend Saved My Life
Nitty Gritty Series, Book Two

Lindsay looks and acts like the perfect fifteen-year-old, but she's hiding a dirty little secret that no amount of fashionista coverings can make better. Telling her mother her step-father is molesting her is not an option. Trying to kill herself again haunts her more than the scars on her wrists, and pretending to be perfect at school might very well drive her over the edge.

Megan knows all about lying. It's been part of her life ever since she realized the only way to escape her poverty-stricken neighborhood was to work hard, keep her mouth shut and wear a mask no one can penetrate. All that changes when Lindsay befriends her.

Can two girls who have little in common discover the value of a real friendship or will the secrets they dare not speak destroy them both?

Off Stroke: How Paddling Saved My Life
Nitty Gritty Series, Book Three

The hard knocks of life keep piling up for Eje. Born into a country on the brink of civil war, he knows the real meaning of survival. After a decade living in Canada, things aren't getting any easier but if he can keep his head down for his last year of high-school he thinks there might be an out for him from his poverty-stricken neighborhood. Too bad fate likes to throw fastballs at Eje and he's forced into an afterschool paddling program. The Aquatic club is filled with white kids, who like to run for fun and paddle for performance. Eje has talent but liking paddling doesn't mean much when you're another kid from the projects.

Shannon used to live to paddle. After a drunk driver crashed into the car holding her and her mother, life has been anything but normal. Re-learning how to kayak isn't fun, and trying to find out where she stands with her once BFFs at the club reinforces how much has changed. Before the accident she'd never give a newbie paddler the time of day, but the minute she meets Eje all that changes. Unlike the guys at the club Eje's mysterious without trying.

When ultimatums threaten to end the afterschool paddle program and secrets get revealed will Eje and Shannon forget their friendship for the good of others or trust each other to do right? Two teens with little in common tackle prejudice and stereotypes to risk it all to help each other.

Off Balance
Nitty Gritty Series, Novella

Jennifer's secret is big but she loves Charlie enough to know ending their teenage relationship will set him free and enable him to join the Army. When Charlie discovers the truth it's up to him to convince Jen their young love was meant to be.

Renee Pace grew up next to the Atlantic Ocean in Nova Scotia, Canada. She writes realistic nitty gritty novels where teenagers come of age and edgy dark teen paranormal novels with strong female characters.

When not writing, she's an active community volunteer. Renee is a member of Romance Writers of Atlantic Canada and a board member of Women in Television & Film in Atlantic Canada.

Her first nitty gritty novel, Off Leash was a semi-finalist in the 2011 Amazon Breakthrough Novel Contest and has been in the Top 100 Amazon Paid ranking for Best Coming of Age story numerous times.

Renee Pace is the penname for Renee Field who writes romance and women fiction novels.

Check out Renee's books at www.reneefield.com.

She can be reached on Facebook at

http://www.facebook.com/ReneePaceYABooks

https://twitter.com/ReneePaceYA

reneepaceauthor@gmail.com

www.ingramcontent.com/pod-product-compliance
Lightning Source LLC
Chambersburg PA
CBHW070633260626
47161CB00007B/2679